I0615043

Sarah Sharp Heaton Hamer

Mrs. Somerville and Mary Carpenter

Sarah Sharp Heaton Hamer

Mrs. Somerville and Mary Carpenter

ISBN/EAN: 9783742812094

Manufactured in Europe, USA, Canada, Australia, Japa

Cover: Foto ©Andreas Hilbeck / pixelio.de

Manufactured and distributed by brebook publishing software
(www.brebook.com)

Sarah Sharp Heaton Hamer

Mrs. Somerville and Mary Carpenter

THE WORLD'S WORKERS.

Mrs. Somerville

AND

Mary Carpenter.

BY

P H Y L L I S _B R O W N E,

Author of "What Girls Can Do," &c.

————— ♦♦♦ —————

C A S S E L L & C O M P A N Y, Limited:

LONDON, PARIS, NEW YORK & MELBOURNE.

[ALL RIGHTS RESERVED.]

1887.

CONTENTS.

MRS. SOMERVILLE.

YOUNG people are generally very much pleased when they can induce old ones to tell stories of their early days ; for the old people remember such curious events. In looking back at the past, they seem to become children again ; they recollect how mischievous they were, and what scrapes they got into. For a while they forget to give advice, or point the moral which adorns their tale.

Some old people enjoy telling these stories as much as the young ones enjoy listening, and some have even of their own accord written down their recollections, for the benefit of those who should come after them. Mrs. Somerville, the subject of this biography, was one of these.

Mrs. Somerville, the grown-up lady, was a great mathematician and philosopher. She was exceedingly clever and accomplished ; she knew a great number of celebrated persons ; and she was very observant, witty, and genial. She was one of the WORLD'S WORKERS, because by her writings she made ignorant readers understand some of the difficult truths of Science. She engaged in studies which before her time had been considered quite beyond the capacity of women, and yet she was a girl at a time when women were not educated as they are now, but spent nearly all their school time in acquiring useless accomplishments. It was owing entirely to her own energy and industry that she accomplished what she did. Her teachers had nothing to do with her success.

Mrs. Somerville lived to be very old. She was ninety-two when she died. During the last years of her life she noted down some of her recollections from early life to old age, and after her death portions of these were published by her daughter. It is from these recollections that we learn what we know of her history.

When speaking of her childhood, it is very amusing to find how very clearly Mrs. Somerville remembered her own feelings and doings as a child. She remembered how terrified she was when she had to go to bed alone in a dark room; how miserable she was at school, "perpetually in tears," and how her schoolfellows used to bathe her eyes in order that the stern schoolmistress might not know that she had been crying; how she used to play at ball and marbles, and was a good deal afraid of a turkey-cock which belonged to a friend of her mother whom she used to visit. In old age she could picture to herself the home she lived in as a girl; the delightful old garden in which she used to wander; the primitive country folk who peopled her youthful

world. Indeed, her memory was so good that her
" Personal Recollections " make a good-sized volume
—one of the most interesting volumes of biography
surely that ever was written.

Into the details of that biography it is impossible
to enter here ; but a brief summary may be given,
and it will be found full of encouragement for other
workers.

Mrs. Somerville was born on the 26th of Decem-
ber, 1780, at Jedburgh, about forty miles south-east
of Edinburgh. She came of a good family; her
father ultimately became Admiral Sir William Fairfax ; he was a descendant of a well-known Yorkshire
family, to which belonged the great Lord Fairfax,
commander-in-chief of the armies of the Parliament
during the civil wars under Charles I.; and her mother
was a Scottish lady, also well connected. Neither of
her parents appears to have been very intellectual,
though they were both possessed of sterling common
sense and great strength of character.

• Little Mary Fairfax was an observant child, with
an intense love of natural objects. She cared nothing
for dolls and toys, like other children, but she loved
the birds and the flowers; she was always eager to watch
the swallows building their nests in the spring, or
preparing for their flight in the autumn. When snow
was on the ground, she used to feed her feathered
favourites, and open the windows to let the robins
hop in and pick crumbs on the breakfast-table. When

her father was at home he was accustomed to spend a good deal of time in the garden, cultivating flowers, for he was an excellent florist, and little Mary learnt from him how to lay carnations, prune fruit trees, and distinguish good plants from worthless ones.

For the most part, however, during the childhood of his daughter, the kind father was away at sea, and Mary was left very much to her own devices. Money was not over plentiful in the household, therefore strict economy had to be observed. During the father's absence, the mother, with her two children, lived at Burntisland, a small seaport on the coast of Fife. The house in which they dwelt must have been a charming old-fashioned residence. It was covered with moss roses in front, and the garden was of a good size, and stretched down to some black rocks which were washed by the sea. It was exactly the sort of place for an original child like Mary to be happy in.

Mary's mother taught her to read, and also to say her prayers morning and evening; but, with this exception, the child's education was much neglected. The Bible was the chief lesson-book, and Mary's mother had a great reverence for the Bible; indeed, she read nothing else, excepting some sermons occasionally and the newspaper. A very curious circumstance, showing this mother's regard for the Bible, seems to have made a great impression on her talented daughter. Mrs. Fairfax was exceedingly afraid of thunder and lightning. When she thought a storm was coming on, she used first to take the steel pins out of her cap, then retire to the far end of the room, and read aloud those sublime poetical descriptions in the Psalms which speak of storms, &c. ; little Mary sitting all the while close by her side, and made more terrified than she otherwise would have been by the sonorous lines. If the storm increased, Mrs. Fairfax would have the window shutters closed, so that she might not see the flashes of lightning; but "though she could no longer see to read, she still kept the Bible on her knee for protection."

That the religious trust (if we may call it so) of Mrs. Fairfax was of rather an extraordinary character was also shown by the following incident, narrated by her daughter : One sunny day, Mrs. Fairfax, who was very much afraid of the sea, was induced to cross the Firth in a boat belonging to a certain skipper in whom she had great confidence. A stiff breeze was blowing, although this was not noticeable so long as the boat was near the shore, but after a few minutes the little craft began to toss and roll. On perceiving this, Mrs. Fairfax called out to the skipper, "George, this is an awful storm. I am sure we are in great danger; mind how you steer. Remember, I trust in you." He laughed and said, "Dinna trust in me, leddy; trust in God Almighty." On hearing this, Mrs. Fairfax, in perfect terror, called out, "Dear me ! Is it come to that ?"

This happy, free life of childhood lasted till Mary was nine years old. Then her father came home from sea, was shocked to find her so ignorant, and arranged for her to be sent to a boarding-school at Musselburgh. Here, as already stated, she was very miserable.

Her experiences ought to be told in her own words. She says :—

"A few days after my arrival at school, although perfectly straight and well made, I was enclosed in stiff stays, with a steel busk in front, while above my frock, bands drew my shoulders back till the shoulder-blades met. Then a steel rod, with a semi-circle which went under my chin, was clasped to the steel busk in my stays. In this constrained state I and most of the younger girls had to prepare our lessons. The chief thing I had to do was to learn by heart a page of Johnson's Dictionary: not only to spell the words, give their parts of speech and meaning, but, as an exercise of memory, to remember their order of succession. Besides, I had to learn the first principles of writing, and the rudiments of French and English grammar. The method of teaching was extremely tedious and inefficient."

People who object to the thorough educational training which girls now enjoy, sometimes speak as if in the old days girls spent the whole of their school time in enjoying themselves, and learning what would fit them to be useful women and good wives and mothers. If we judge by this account which Mrs. Somerville has given, the school girls of former times had their trials, while the results obtained were not at all satisfactory.

Nor must we imagine that Mrs. Somerville had an experience uncommon in those days. Miss Edgeworth lived at the same time as Mrs. Somerville, and in her life we read that, being sent to a certain fashionable establishment, "she underwent all the usual tortures of back-boards, iron collars and dumbs, and also (because she was always a very tiny person) the unusual one of being hung by the neck to draw out the muscles and increase the growth —a signal failure in her case."

But the trying ordeal of school-life for Mary only lasted a year. At the end of that time she returned home, but she was woefully ignorant. According to her own confession, her writing was as bad as possible. When called upon to write a short reply to a letter, she could neither compose the answer nor spell the words. Very naturally, her mother was exceedingly dissatisfied. She said that she would have been contented if Mary had only learnt to write well and keep accounts, which was all that a woman was expected to know.

But, notwithstanding her deficiencies, it was decided that Mary should remain at home for good, "and it was arranged that a large portion of her time should be devoted to domestic concerns."

Besides this, she had her sampler, that important achievement of the properly brought up young lady of the period, to work. Yet after all her duties were done, she had leisure for her own pursuits. When left to herself, it was her delight to wander along the sea-shore, collecting shells, sea-weeds, and sea-fowls' eggs. When the tide was low she took off her shoes and stockings and waded among the rocks, watching the crabs and marine animals ; she took long rambles inland too, and made herself familiar with the local names of the ferns and wild flowers. On the blocks of limestone which were brought from the neighbouring country to the little pier she noticed marks of what seemed like the forms of leaves, but she had no idea that these were fossils, and guessed nothing of the glimpses they gave into conditions long passed away.

Bad weather was a great trial to Mary Fairfax. At first she did not know how to occupy herself when it occurred ; but after a time, to her great delight, she discovered a small collection of books, one of which was a "Shakespeare." These were eagerly taken possession of and read at every spare moment. Mary's mother did not prevent her from reading, but evidently she did not approve of a girl "wasting her time thus." So when a rather terrible "Aunt Janet" appeared on the scene and expostulated, the girl was sent to the village school to learn plain needlework. But the mischief was done. The taste for reading

was acquired, never to be lost again. The tiny
seed from which would grow the glorious harvest
of knowledge that was to astonish the generation,
lay hidden in that "small collection of books, one
of which was Shakespeare," discovered in the old
country house at Burntisland.

Housewives in Scotland were very proud of their
house linen in those days. Country gentlefolk grew
the flax on their estates, which their maids spun; the
coarser yarn being woven close at hand, and the
finer sort usually sent to a manufactory. Mrs. Fairfax was a notable housewife in this respect. She
had a goodly supply of linen, and some of it was very
fine and beautiful. Doubtless she devoted much of
her time to making and mending it. This would
make her all the more grieved when she found that
her daughter cared for reading more than for sewing.
But it turned out that the daughter could sew as well
as read. She learned to love needlework; and when,
after a time, the linen for some very fine shirts was
put into her hands, Mary made one shirt all by herself so well, that her mother felt there was no further
ground for uneasiness about skill with the needle, and
that, while she might safely be relieved from attending
the village school, she might with equal safety be
put in charge of the linen press. It is pleasant to
find that the accomplishment thus gained Mrs. Somerville retained through life. She left behind her some
most elaborate specimens of embroidery and lace work.

The occupation of sewing, however, had not destroyed the passion for knowledge, and little by little Mary overcame the obstacles which stood in the way of her becoming possessed of it. All her friends and acquaintance disapproved of her devotion to study, but they could not stop her career. She commenced a course of history unaided; she made the most of the little French she had learnt at school, and practised French translation; and she attempted to teach herself Latin. She even persuaded her mother to allow the village schoolmaster to teach her the use of the terrestrial and celestial globes. The last-named study was specially to her taste. On starlight nights she would sit for hours at her bedroom window, gazing at that starlit sky whose wonders it was to be the work of her life to explain to others.

Music, too, possessed great charms for Mary Fairfax, and in the early part of her life she gave a good deal of time to it. When she was about thirteen, an uncle, coming over from India, made her a present of a piano, and the presentation of the gift led to her taking music lessons. Indeed, for a considerable period she used to practise four or five hours a day, and rose early in order that she might do so. At first, she tells us, she had a bad habit of thumping the piano, and so breaking the strings. This was awkward, especially as there was no piano-tuner in the village where she lived, and she had to learn to mend the broken strings and tune the instrument herself.

But she was always too shy to do herself justice in performing before strangers. To the last day of her life Beethoven was her favourite composer.

A very bright spot in the memory of the Mary Somerville, the great mathematician and elderly lady, was a visit which Mary Fairfax, the girl of thirteen, paid to Dr. and Mrs. Somerville, her uncle and aunt, at Jedburgh. This Dr. Somerville was the father of the Mr. William Somerville who afterwards became Mary's husband. Dr. Somerville's house—the Manse, as it was called—was a charming place. It stood in the midst of a large garden, well stocked with fruit-trees, flowers, and vegetables. A pure stream flowed through the valley which lay beyond the Manse garden, and here Mary and her cousins used to bathe. Sometimes they went nutting in the forest, sometimes they went on expeditions, looking for birds. But all these delights sank into insignificance beside the greatest of all, which was that Mary found sympathy and encouragement to study in her uncle's house.

Her cousins had little love for books, but her aunt was a great reader, and Shakespeare—Mary's friend, Shakespeare—was her favourite author. Her uncle, too, was a most genial, talented man. He did what he could to encourage his niece in her pursuit of knowledge. When, rendered bold by his kindness, she ventured to confess to him that she had tried to teach herself Latin, but feared that she would never make much progress, he advised her to persevere, and told her that in ancient times many women of the highest rank had been elegant Latin scholars. Moreover, he promised that if she would come to him every morning before breakfast for an hour or two, he would help her with her lessons. All this was quite a change for Mary. Hitherto her friends had disapproved of her devotion to study, and had reproved her for it. Can we wonder that in old age she said, " I never was happier in my life than during the months I spent at Jedburgh."

For some time after this the history of Mary Fairfax is made up of the recapitulation of the subjects of study which, one after another, she took up. She learned to draw, and "actually wasted time in copying prints." Later, she had an opportunity of attending an academy presided over by Nasmyth, an exceedingly good landscape painter. Her own estimate of her performances was modest enough. " I spoilt canvas," she said, " but I had made some progress by the end of the season." Many years afterwards, however, the master told a lady of his acquaintance that " the cleverest young lady he ever taught was Miss Mary Fairfax."

About the same time, too, she began to learn Greek, and took a keen interest in the politics of the day. Indeed, it was a characteristic of the future Mrs. Somerville that when she was a girl she never allowed herself to miss an opportunity of learning.

No matter whether the subject in hand seemed likely to be immediately useful or not, if it came within her reach, she perseveringly and industriously tried to make it her own. It was this faculty of hers which was the basis of her future greatness, and which enabled her, humanly speaking, to work out her career. It has been the repeated experience of students that it is never safe to neglect opportunities which come in the way of gaining what seem to be the most unusual pieces of knowledge. Once acquired, patiently and thoroughly, such knowledge is certain to prove useful sooner or later, whilst if the occasion for taking hold of it is allowed to pass, it is equally certain to be wanted at some time or other. Mary Fairfax never made the mistake of letting treasures of information slip away from her because she failed to lay hold of them.

Yet it would be a mistake to imagine that this period of girlhood was entirely given up to hard study and application. The contrary was the case. Soon after leaving the Manse, Mary paid a visit to the house of another uncle who lived at Edinburgh, and while there she attended a dancing-class, and went into society to some extent. But she did not breathe freely in this sort of atmosphere, and probably was very glad when, the winter being over, she returned to the old home at Burntisland. Although she did not know it, she was now approaching a crisis in her life, for she was about to make acquaintance with the

B

subject which was to interest her more than anything else, and through familiarity with which she was to become famous. This subject was Algebra ; but until this time Mary Fairfax was entirely ignorant of it.

Mary's introduction to algebra was made very curiously. As a matter of course, the young lady went with her mother to the tea-parties which used to be very frequently given in the sort of social circle to which Mrs. Fairfax belonged. As might have been expected, Mary did not enjoy these gatherings. She found them very tedious ; and when fortunate enough to meet with young companions of her own age, she was doubtless glad to escape for an hour from the society of her elders, and to talk of something else than cards.

One day when she had escaped in this way, she went off with a young friend—Miss Ogilvie by name—to look at some fancy-work done by the latter. After these elegant trifles had been duly admired, a certain monthly magazine was brought out, with coloured plates of ladies' dresses, charades, and puzzles. The two girls examined these, and then——. But the incident shall be told in Mrs. Somerville's own words :

"At the end of a page I read what appeared to me to be simply an arithmetical question, but on turning the page, I was surprised to see strange-looking lines mixed with letters, chiefly x's and y's, and asked ' What is that ? ' ' Oh,' said Miss Ogilvie, ' it is a kind of arithmetic ; they call it algebra, but I can tell you nothing about it.' And we talked about other things ; but on going home, I thought I would look if any of our books could tell me what was meant by algebra. In Robertson's " Navigation " I flattered myself that I had got precisely what I wanted ; but I soon found that I was mistaken. I perceived, however, that astronomy did not consist in star-gazing, and as I persevered in studying the book for a time, I certainly got a dim view of several sub-jects which were useful to me afterwards. Unfor-tunately, not one of our acquaintances or relations knew anything of science or natural history, nor, had they done so, should I have had courage to ask any of them a question, for I should have been laughed at. I was often very sad and forlorn ; not a hand held out to help me."

Yet most girls of the age of Mary Fairfax, in like circumstances with herself, would have thought they had quite enough to do without troubling further. At the time when she was thus longing to study algebra, Mary was giving four or five hours a day to music ; she was practising drawing very energetically, and was keeping up her other studies ; she was taking part in household affairs, and was making and mending her own clothes. Also she went into society, was particu-larly fond of going to the theatre, and never missed an opportunity of seeing Shakespeare acted. Last, but not least, she went every day to a pastry-cook's, with a companion, to learn the art of cookery, utilising

B 2

the knowledge thus gained by preparing with her own hands the jellies and creams required for the little supper-parties given by her mother.

The fact that this greatest woman-mathematician of any age was a skilful cook and a clever needle-woman ought to be specially noted. Some people have an idea that intellectual women must of necessity be helpless with their hands. It has been proved again and again that this is a mistake. The truth of the matter is that the capacity which enables a woman to cultivate her mind renders it easy for her to fulfil domestic duties also. Experience bears us out when we say that it is a libel on women of education and talent to say that they cannot be skilful house-wives; and the libel has partly arisen from the fact that clever women find housekeeping so easy that they do it without saying much about it. When a young lady is likely to be called upon to preside over a home, the point of importance for those who are going to be dependent upon her for their comfort is not what she knows, but what she is. If she is industrious, energetic, clear-headed, and practical, the probability is that as a housekeeper she will soon far surpass the girl who is lackadaisical and limp, even though the latter has practised nothing but cookery, house-keeping, and needlework ever since she could walk.

Mrs. Somerville, the great philosopher and mathe-matician, is a proof that culture is not incompatible with housewifely skill. Miss Cobbe, who was her

friend and correspondent for many years, has testified
that Mrs. Somerville was renowned for her good
housekeeping, and "an excellent judge of a well-
dressed *déjeuner* and of choice old sherry." In a
paper read before the Social Science Congress on
the education of women, Miss Cobbe remarked :—
"The woman whose home was the happiest I ever
saw; whose aged husband (as I have many times
heard him) rose up and called her blessed above all,
whose children were amongst the most devoted, was
the same woman who in her youth outstripped nearly
all the men of her time in the paths of science, and
who in her beloved and honoured age still studied
reverently the wonders of God's creation. That
woman was Mary Somerville."

The practice of cookery, however, did not put
algebra out of court, for Mary Fairfax was not the
sort of person to allow herself to be discouraged. She
said of herself, "I never lost sight of an object which
had interested me from the first."

One day, when she was having her drawing lesson,
she heard Mr. Nasmyth talking to some ladies about
perspective. He said to them, "You should study
Euclid's Elements of Geometry : the foundation not
only of perspective, but also of astronomy and all
mechanical science."

Here was the suggestion that was wanted. Advantage could not, however, be immediately taken of it,
as " Euclid's Elements " was nowhere to be found, and

Mary never entertained the idea of going into a bookseller's and ordering it. Yet the title of the work was remembered, and when, later, it was discovered that Mary's brother was in need of a tutor, and a gentleman named Mr. Craw was chosen to fill the situation, Mary ventured to consult him about her studies, and asked if the first time he went to Edinburgh he would buy for her the books she needed. He did so, and thus she became possessed of what she had so long desired. She set to work with a will, and, except for a little occasional help good-naturedly given by Mr. Craw, studied alone with determination and assiduity, worked out algebraical problems, gradually forming an acquaintance with those great natural laws which are the key to so much that is mysterious in the story of the heavenly bodies.

Mary was so busy before she began Euclid that it is not astonishing that she found a little difficulty in making the new study " fit in " with all her other work. Already she rose early that she might find time for practising music ; now she found it necessary to sit up late for algebra. This habit was eventually put a stop to, not because it was too much for the girl, but because it caused the consumption of too many candles. " The servants complained that it was no wonder the stock of candles was soon exhausted, for Miss Mary sat up reading till a late hour." So orders were given that Miss Mary's candle should be taken away as soon as she was in bed.

When Mary could no longer work out her problems on paper, she did them in her mind, and every night she worked out from memory a number of problems which had been already gone through. But, as on a former occasion, it was her father who discovered that all was not right, and interfered to make it so. When Mary was running wild and learning nothing at all, her father had said, "This kind of life will never do. Mary must at least know how to write and keep accounts," so she had been sent to boarding-school. This time the danger was of a different sort ; Mary was studying too hard, her father said. "We must put a stop to this, or we shall have Mary in a strait jacket one of these days." In both cases the father's interference was beneficial.

Strange to say, the first of her pursuits which brought honour to Mary was painting. She had worked very hard under Mr. Nasmyth, and had not only copied several landscapes he had lent her, but had ventured on a little original execution by colouring the outline of a print from an actual storm witnessed from the garden. A friend of the family, Dr. Blair, the kindly minister of the High Kirk in Edinburgh, heard of the girl's skill, and asked permission to look at the contents of her portfolio. A few pictures were sent to him, and in a day or two he returned them with a letter addressed to Mary herself, and containing words of high praise.

Naturally the girl was very proud of this appreciation, but her satisfaction was not permitted to be
entirely without alloy. A wealthy connection of the
Fairfaxes, named Mrs. Ramsay, one of those amiable
individuals who find satisfaction in taking the gilt off
another person's gingerbread, came one day to the
house to pay a call, and looking round the room, asked
who had painted the pictures hung on the wall. It
was explained that Mary was the artist. " I am glad,"
said Mrs. Ramsay, " that Mary Fairfax has any kind
of talent that may enable her to win her bread, for
every one knows that she will not have a sixpence."

Until this moment the idea of making money had
never entered Mary's mind. In narrating the
anecdote afterwards, however, she characteristically
remarked, " Had it been my lot to win my bread by
painting, I should never have been ashamed of it. I
was intensely ambitious to excel in something, for
I felt in my own breast that women were capable
of taking a higher place in creation than that assigned
to them in my early days, which was very low."

However, Mary Fairfax was not called upon at
this period to " win her bread," for when she was
about twenty-four years of age she married Mr.
Samuel Greig, a distant relation of her mother's family.

Yet it must not be supposed that she married
before she had had a taste of the pleasures of
girlhood. For two or three years before she
settled down as Mrs. Greig, she went a good deal

into society. She was very pretty, and had a refined and delicate kind of beauty, which won universal admiration; indeed, amongst her companions she went by the name of "The Rose of Jedwood." Although her friends were comparatively poor, they belonged to the upper strata of society, and she received plenty of invitations to join in whatever gaiety was going. True, her mother made it a rule to refuse to go into public during her father's absence; but Mary never felt the want of a chaperon. Several lady friends she had who were quite willing to take charge of her, and girls were allowed abundant liberty in that pleasant Edinburgh society of the period. *Bonâ fide* balls were not common, but friendly supper-parties were very usual, and to these the partners of the previous evening were admitted, and presented by the young ladies to their parents. Games, music, and even a little quiet dancing, were the amusements on these occasions, and it was the fashion for the girls to propose a toast or a sentiment to be approved by the guests. Mary Fairfax seldom ventured to give a toast: she was too timid to obtrude herself upon her friends thus; but she enjoyed hearing what others had to say, and thoroughly entered into the spirit of the entertainment. It is to be noted that she always made her own dresses for these festive gatherings.

Though thus mixing in society, Mary never abandoned what she had taught herself to regard as the chief object of her life—the prosecution of her studies. Still she practised music diligently, still she continued to paint, and still she took her part in domestic affairs ; and as all this left very little time for her beloved algebra, she resolved to rise every morning at daybreak and work problems or classics till breakfast-time. This method answered admirably, and many an hour Mary Fairfax thus gave to study, sitting meanwhile in her bed wrapped in a blanket, on account of the cold. Can we wonder that she made rapid progress?

Part of her method of work is well worth the attention of young students. While studying, she studied most diligently, but she found again and again that after reading for a certain time, and becoming fatigued to a certain point, she seemed to lose the power of fixing her attention. When this feeling came over her she invariably stopped at once, and took up something fresh ; for she tells us that if, feeling unnerved and fagged, she tried to continue reading, she did more harm than good ; but if she turned away from study entirely for a time, she returned to it in a little while fresh and eager. School girls would do well to remember the experience of Mary Fairfax in this way. No greater mistake can be made when learning lessons than to pore over a book after one has become bewildered and dazed. The sensation of discomfort is Nature's hint that work has gone on long enough, and that it is time for play. Nature's hints can never be disregarded without unpleasant consequences, and the girl who refuses to act upon them will not only injure her health, but lessen her capacity for work.

Our student soon found this out, and after one or two painful experiences she did what girls in her position will always find to be wisest and best. As soon as ever she realised that her brain was refusing to attend closely and reason clearly, she ceased to make demands upon it. Immediately she put aside her task, and took up either a story-book or a piece of needle-work. Poetry was her great resource at these times. Novels, too, she read with interest, and, strangest of all, ghost stories and witch stories.

If it should be thought incredible that a highly-educated woman, such as Mary Fairfax afterwards became, should at any time of her life have felt the slightest interest in ghostly legends, we must recall to mind that times then were different from times now. Then the common people all believed in apparitions, and even the upper classes felt an unpleasant tremor when darkness came on and found them near a churchyard, or alone in one of the many places which then had a reputation for being uncanny. Mrs. Somerville in later life was accustomed to tell of a naval officer, a friend of hers, who doubtless was brave as a lion when brought face to face with real dangers. This gentle-man confessed that he never opened his eyes after he was once in bed. He was asked why. "For fear I should see something," was the reply. Brought up in this atmosphere, it is not astonishing that superstition possessed a certain fascination even over a girl so far in advance of her time as was the then Mary Fairfax. That the ghost stories produced their effect, however, is very evident. Even when quite an old lady, after she had entered her eighty-ninth year, Mrs. Somerville confessed that "she was afraid to sleep alone on a stormy night, and could not sleep comfortably any night unless some one was near."

Mary was twice married. Her first husband—Mr. Samuel Greig—had little sympathy with his young wife's love of science, and the three years during which she lived with him must have been rather dreary and uninteresting. Before his marriage, Mr. Greig had been in the employ of the Russian Government, but as Russia was at that period by no means a desirable residence for foreigners, Mary's father would not entertain the idea of her living there, and only consented to the marriage when the intended bridegroom obtained the appointment of Russian Consul in England, and had to settle in London.

To London, therefore, Mary went. Of course she had no fortune, and on account of the poverty of her family her wedding trousseau was a very modest one. When she left home, however, her mother managed to put twenty pounds into her hands, telling her that with this sum she was to buy a shawl or something warm for winter.

But Mary ascertained that the President of the Academy of Painting had just painted a portrait of her father—her own dear father, who shortly before had distinguished himself greatly at the battle of Camperdown, been knighted, and made a colonel of Marines, and of whom she was exceedingly proud. Mary was asked to go and see the portrait. She went, and liked it very much, and inquired the price. It was twenty pounds. The temptation was too great. The "something warm for winter" was given up, and in its place Mary became the possessor of her father's likeness. What her mother said to this purchase we do not know, but Mrs. Somerville did not regret it, and the painting is still in the possession of her family—a pleasant proof of a daughter's love.

Mary's new home was very different from the delightful old house at Burntisland, with its ivy-covered walls and spacious garden. It was a small house, badly ventilated, situated near a London square, in which Mary could walk, if so inclined. Her husband was away all day, and at first she knew scarcely any one, though after a time she made one or two agreeable acquaintances, in visiting whom she found a little change. But as a rule, she spent much of her time alone, and very naturally she returned to her scientific pursuits.

Her husband had a very low opinion of the mental power of women, and he had neither knowledge of nor interest in science of any kind; but he did not prevent her from studying. She worked, however, under great disadvantages ; and after a time two babies came into the home, and doubtless they diverted their mother's attention from mathematics. Yet it was during this rather trying period that she managed to master French, and learnt to speak it so as to be understood. Mary's residence in London was very brief. After three years, Mr. Greig died, and his widow, with her two little sons, returned to her father's home. In a short time the younger child died also. The elder one, Woronzow Greig, lived to be a great comfort to his mother.

The next five years of Mary's life were given up almost entirely to study. The death of her husband and her baby had saddened the poor lady, and she was very glad to turn for consolation to those pursuits which in time past had given her so much satisfaction. She was independent now, being possessed of a fair income, and she was at liberty to please herself. Her friends hoped that she would have given entertainments and lived a life of gaiety, but her tastes did not lie in this direction. She attempted no concealment, was quite indifferent about being considered eccentric and foolish ; she made her plans and consistently adhered to them. She entered upon a systematic course of study in mathematics and astronomy, and devoted a certain number of hours each day to reading, and she even engaged a tutor to help her with her books, although she soon found that she knew as

much as he did. In the evening she played piquet
with her father, or practised music. Ordinary individuals find it rather appalling to go over the list of
her achievements; but they ought to remember that
the student was by no means an ordinary individual.

One or two characteristics of this great woman
ought not to be passed over in silence. In reading
her "Recollections," we rarely find her giving any information about her personal feelings during the
solemn crises of life. Her marriage, the birth of her
children, the bereavements she had to endure, and
similar events, are passed over with a mere mention of
the date of their occurrence.

She was a woman of strong affections, and of course
no one could live to a great age, as she did, without
having to go through sorrow ; but she shrank from
making a display of her feelings. In opinion, too,
she was very broad and liberal. When quite young,
she dared to think for herself, and rejected beliefs
which science taught her were incompatible with the
greatness and goodness of the Creator. Yet she had a
very clear and simple faith, which influenced every
thought and action of her life. But she did not care
to talk in general company either about religion or
about her own affairs ; and she specially directed her
daughter to suppress everything in her "Recollections"
which would merely gratify curiosity. The consequence is, that though we hear all about her studies, and
about the interesting people whom she met, we hear

little of her thoughts in joy and sorrow. In one way this is to be regretted. Sorrow and pain come alike to all, and it might have helped those who are in the thick of the fight if they could have heard how it was that this brave soldier bore herself so valiantly.

It was after her return to Scotland, and when she was thirty-three years of age, that Mrs. Somerville first became possessed of a small library. Hitherto, she had had to struggle on as best she might, getting a volume here and another there, as she was able. But now, having both means and time at her disposal, and having friends whom she could consult, she obtained from the then Professor of Mathematics in the University of Edinburgh a list of works likely to be of service, and these she bought straight away. Some of these books were in French, some in Latin, and all would have been looked upon as entirely profound and difficult by the majority of ladies. But Mary was delighted with her little library. She says, " I could hardly believe that I possessed such a treasure when I looked back on the day that I first saw the mysterious word 'Algebra,' and the long course of years in which I had persevered, almost without hope. It taught me never to despair. I now pursued my studies with increased assiduity."

It is very interesting to note that these books, and all the other mathematical works belonging to Mrs. Somerville, were at her death presented to the Women's College at Girton, Cambridge.

Mr. William Somerville, the great mathematician's second husband, was her cousin, the son of that very Rev. Dr. Somerville who had encouraged her when a girl in the pursuit of knowledge. Mr. Somerville belonged to a very well-known Scottish family, whose history, entitled " Memorie of the Somervilles " (written by James, eleventh Lord Somerville, who died in 1690), had been edited by Sir Walter Scott. Mr. Somerville himself was a most kindly, genial man. He was most devotedly attached to his talented wife, regarded her with the most intense admiration, and did all he could to encourage her to study. He very generously acknowledged that she was intellectually his superior, and was most proud and gratified when her talents were appreciated, and honours were showered upon her. He helped her in her work in every way that was open to him, and even made it his business to look out the books she required, and to copy her manuscripts. The marriage was an exceedingly happy one, and the most perfect confidence existed between husband and wife. Although as a mathematician Mrs. Somerville was without doubt the more advanced of the two, in practical matters Mr. Somerville was the leader, and his wife trusted in him entirely, and regarded him with the deepest affection. A beautiful trait in Mrs. Somerville's character was that modesty which led her to refrain from making parade of her attainments. Her manners were simple and natural, and she never laid claim to

C

superior knowledge. Her temper was humble and gentle, and these qualities made her loved by all who came under her influence.

Very naturally, knowing the lady intimately, as he did, and having had opportunity to note her talents and beautiful character, Dr. Somerville, Mary's old friend, was exceedingly gratified when it was decided that his son should marry his favourite niece. His wife too, Mary's aunt, the aunt who had sympathised with her in her admiration for Shakespeare, was very anxious that a union should be effected between the two.

But the other members of the Somerville family were not equally satisfied. As one consequence of her zealous devotion to study, the bride had gained for herself a reputation for eccentricity, and her tastes were criticised by her neighbours with extreme severity. Most probably it was taken for granted that because the young lady was clever and fond of books, therefore she could not be domesticated, and would make a bad wife. So strong and bitter was the dislike which her ability had aroused, that one of Mr. Somerville's sisters, who was unmarried, and younger than her intended sister-in-law, wrote a most impertinent letter to her new relative, in which she said, " I hope you will now give up your foolish manner of life and studies, and make a respectable and useful wife to my brother."

An epistle of this kind was not calculated to

arouse kindly feelings, and the newly-married pair were exceedingly indignant on receiving it.

But an amusing incident soon made these critical relatives see that the new wife was not the helpless " blue-stocking " that she was supposed to be.

When the pair were married, they went to the English Lakes on their honeymoon trip, and rather to their discomfiture, a sister Janet of Mr. Somerville's insisted on accompanying them ; while shortly after, a brother Samuel and his wife followed Janet's example. It is not often that a bride has to entertain her husband's relatives on her wedding tour ; yet such was Mrs. Somerville's lot. But this was not all. The queerly-assorted party had not been in their holiday quarters more than a day or two before Brother Samuel was taken ill of a fever, which mishap led to the whole party being detained in Cumberland for a month. During his illness he had a longing for some currant jelly, and the person who offered to make it for him was the much despised learned bride. In telling this anecdote, Mrs. Somerville says, " I never can forget the astonishment expressed at my being able to be so useful."

Once more Mary, the newly-married, settled in London, and once more she began her new life by taking up a fresh study. Her former husband had, however, simply permitted her efforts ; this one encouraged her in making them, and even suggested subjects to her. When a tutor had to be engaged

C 2

for his step-son, Woronzow Greig, Mr. Somerville recommended his wife to take advantage of the opportunity, and renew her acquaintance with Greek; and Mrs. Somerville, acting on the hint, read "Homer" for an hour every morning before breakfast. Then it was discovered that the Greek master understood botany, so, once more following her husband's advice, the lady devoted an hour every morning to that science, "though she was nursing a baby at the time." Not many mothers with small babies would have ventured to attempt so much.

Mineralogy was the next subject mastered by this wonderful woman; and this the husband and wife took up together with the greatest interest. Whilst on a tour which they made on the Continent, they went to see some silver mines, and the specimens of minerals there obtained reminded Mrs. Somerville that she had some time before seen at a friend's house a magnificent collection of precious and curious metals. She told her husband of this, and he proposed that they should work together and make a collection. A view of the fossils preserved in the Edinburgh Museum then recalled the fossil plants brought from the coal mines to the small pier at Burntisland, and ultimately geology was mastered. Thus, little by little, the store of knowledge grew.

After all this study and industry, it would have been thought that Mrs. Somerville would have been

the last person in the world who needed to deplore her
own "deficiencies." Yet it is a proof of her modesty
that she did so ; and one of her chief anxieties when
her children were young was to engage foreign
nurses and governesses for them, so that " they never
might have to undergo the embarrassment and
mortification from which she had suffered from ignorance of the common European languages." Yet
it will be remembered that the lady had taken great
pains to learn French, and that she read nearly all her
scientific works in that language, though she could
not speak it fluently. Also, when in Italy she engaged a lady to converse with her in Italian every
day, and so was able to understand it when spoken,
and to be able to keep up a conversation in the
language, though not to speak it well. One of the
" mortifications" which were caused by her supposed
" ignorance " is worth recording. When in Florence,
Mrs. Somerville was on one occasion presented to
the Countess of Albany, the widow of Prince Charles
Edward Stuart, the Pretender. After talking a little,
the countess said, " So you don't speak Italian. You
must have had a very bad education." Seeing that
this remark was addressed to the woman who was
perhaps more highly educated than ever woman had
been before, it may be pronounced amusing as well
as impertinent.

About this time Mrs. Somerville had the great
grief to lose her father. He was a good man, of a

brave and noble nature, and his great daughter was devotedly attached to him. He served in the British Navy sixty-seven years, and was seventy-seven years old when he died.

For some years after her second marriage Mrs. Somerville devoted herself to her family, to her friends, and to the thousand and one duties and pleasures which go to make up the life of a lady of good position. She and her husband lived part of the time in London, and partly in Scotland, paying occasional visits to the Continent. They led a very happy, cheerful life, and numbered amongst their acquaintance some of the men and women of the time best worth knowing, both in England and abroad.

Sir Walter Scott was an intimate friend of the Somervilles, and a charming set of people met for some time in the neighbourhood of Abbotsford, Sir Walter's residence. Mrs. Somerville used in after life to speak quite enthusiastically of the pleasant supper-parties enjoyed at Abbotsford, when Scott would be the life of the party, telling amusing stories and ghost and witch legends.

At these parties it was usual for one or two of the guests to sing comic songs, and the others vied with each other in the display of wit. When the time came for the company to disperse, it was usual for all present to rise and join hands round the table, then Scott, taking the lead, they sang—

" Weel may we a' be,
Ill may we never see ;
Health to the King
And the gude companie."

A very amusing circumstance in connection with Mrs. Somerville's acquaintance with Sir Walter arose out of the childish inquisitiveness of Woronzow Greig, Mrs. Somerville's little boy.

During the time Mrs. Somerville was visiting Abbotsford, the " Waverley Novels" were appearing, and were creating a great sensation ; yet even Scott's intimate friends did not know that he was the author ; he enjoyed keeping the affair a mystery. But little Woronzow discovered what he was about. One day when Mrs. Somerville was talking about a novel that had just been published, Woronzow said, " I knew all these stories long ago, for Mr. Scott writes on the dinner-table ; when he has finished he puts the green cloth with the papers in a corner of the dining-room, and when he goes out Charlie Scott and I read the stories."

This incident shows what has been shown many a time before and since : that persons who want to keep a secret ought to be very careful when children are about.

Not only Sir Walter, however, but Sir David Brewster, Sir William and Lady Herschel, Dr. Marcet and his wife, the authoress of the "Conversations on Chemistry," the Rev. Sydney Smith, Rogers,

Thomas Moore, Campbell, Macaulay, Sir James Mackintosh, and professors, authors, and scientists without number, were in their prime at that time, and Mr. and Mrs. Somerville met them frequently in society.

But, indeed, to go through the list of persons known to the Somervilles is like going through a list of the literary celebrities of the time. Those who knew her well, however, have told us that Mrs. Somerville was always very quiet and modest in her behaviour at these gatherings. She was naturally timid, and quite unable to argue in public, even when she knew that she was right. "The only thing," she says, "in which I was determined and inflexible was the prosecution of my studies. They were perpetually interrupted, but always resumed at the first opportunity. I do not think I err much in saying that perseverance is a characteristic of mine."

A great sorrow now befell the Somervilles. Their eldest daughter, a lovely and affectionate girl, was taken ill, and after suffering for a long time, died. Mrs. Somerville had already lost several children, but they had, for the most part, died in infancy. This young girl was intelligent beyond her years, and specially dear to both her parents. The event is of interest to us, because in connection with it we are allowed one glimpse into the mother's feelings. A little while after her daughter was taken from her, Mrs. Somerville wrote to her father-in-law, Dr.

Somerville, and the letter is published in her "Recollections." In it Mrs. Somerville says—

"Even in the bitterness of my soul I acknowledge the wisdom and goodness of God, and endeavour to be resigned to His will. It is ungrateful not to remember the many happy years we have enjoyed, but that very remembrance renders our present state more desolate and dreary. The great source of consolation is in the mercy of God, and the virtues of those we lament ; the full assurance that no good disposition can be lost, but must be brought to perfection in a better world. Our business is to render ourselves fit for that blessed inheritance, that we may again be united to those we mourn."

Mrs. Somerville is not the first mother who has found comfort in bereavement in remembering the goodness of her lost darling, and in looking forward to a blessed re-union.

Hitherto Mrs. Somerville had been occupied only in acquiring knowledge, but now the time was approaching when she was to put knowledge within the reach of others. This was the period of her true greatness ; for men and women are only really great when they give. Knowledge kept entirely to oneself, and not applied in any way, is not worth very much, but knowledge communicated and made useful is of the greatest value.

Some months before this, Dr. Wollaston, a celebrated chemist, and one of Mrs. Somerville's most intimate friends, came to see her. On entering the room he said, " I have discovered seven dark lines crossing the solar spectrum, which I want to show you ;" then closing the window shutters so as to leave only a narrow line of light, he put a small glass prism into her hand, and told her to look. She did so, and at once perceived what her friend pointed out.

She was very pleased and proud when she found that she was the first person to whom Dr. Wollaston showed these lines, as the discovery proved to be of great importance. It does not seem improbable that it was this circumstance which led Mrs. Somerville to give special consideration to the solar rays. Whether this be so or not, it is a fact that her first important contribution to science was made in the form of a paper read before the Royal Society, in which she tried to show that the violet rays in the solar spectrum have a magnetic influence. Her theory led to much discussion, although it was not ultimately established. Still it was useful, because it led to important investigations.

This paper, together with other more fragmentary ones, had already made Mrs. Somerville known as a practical astronomer, and she was not permitted to hide her light.

One day, some months after the production of the paper on the solar rays, Mrs. Somerville was much startled to hear that her husband had received a letter from Lord Brougham, asking him to try and use his influence to persuade her to write a popular account of a book which had for some years past completely revolutionised people's ideas about the science of astronomy. This work, called "La Mécanique Céleste," had been written by Laplace, a Frenchman, one of the greatest mathematicians and astronomers who ever lived, and whose discoveries had earned for him the title of the Newton of France. When Lord Brougham wrote this letter Lapiace was just dead, and the cleverest men in Europe were enthusiastic in his praise ; yet scientific men in England had to confess that there were not twenty Englishmen who knew of his great book at all, except by name, and not a hundred who had ever heard of it. The fact was, the "Mécanique Céleste" was beyond the comprehension of ordinary people. It was so difficult to understand that no one who had not a profound knowledge of geometry could possibly read it ; and it was said that, when writing it, the author himself used sometimes to be obliged to devote an hour's labour to gathering up the thread which he had dropped when last he wrote.

Abstruse as the work was, Mrs. Somerville had mastered its contents. She had read it with great interest, and when in France she had made the acquaintance of Laplace, and conversed with him about astronomy : indeed, Laplace is reported to have said that Mrs. Somerville was the only woman who understood his work. And, seeing that the book itself was a work of great genius, that it contained such wonderful revelations of the way in which the planets, "tumbling down their orbits, were really obeying the law of gravitation," Lord Brougham felt that it would be an immense advantage if only a few people could, by the help of Mrs. Somerville, be added to those who honoured and were indebted to the great Frenchman.

When subjects are very difficult in themselves, and have been discussed in learned languages only, it is not at all an easy business to attempt to state them clearly in simple language. This Mrs. Somerville knew quite well, and when Lord Brougham made the proposal, she was surprised beyond expression, and said at once that she felt quite incapable of doing work of the kind proposed. However, Lord Brougham persisted, and her husband joined him in trying to persuade her at least to make an attempt, and see what she could do. So at last she consented to try, on two conditions : first, that the affair should be kept secret ; and secondly, that if, after doing her best, her best was found to be a failure, the manuscript should be put in the fire, and not another word said about the matter.

From this period the entire course of Mrs. Somerville's life was changed. Hitherto her time had been fully occupied in looking after her household, taking care of, and even educating, her children, going out

into society, and giving what time she could spare to
study. But now she had a definite work to do, and
she made arrangements accordingly. She did not
neglect her family and children ; she still continued to
educate the latter ; indeed, it was her practice whilst
writing her books to keep her two little girls in the
room with her, and to superintend their lessons at
intervals. This fact alone shows what a powerful
mind she had. As a rule, literary people find it
necessary to have perfect quiet while they are at
work. They cannot bear the least interruption, and
become quite irritable when they are disturbed. But
mothers who undertake to write cannot secure lux-
urious conditions like these. They must either leave
their little ones to strangers, or they must get into the
way of thinking and working to themselves, so as not
to be concerned in what goes on around them. The
habit is most difficult to acquire, yet it has been
acquired again and again, and Mrs. Somerville was
capable of gaining it.

Her daughter tells us that whilst she was busy at
work talking went on in the same room ; the children
practised their scales, and learnt their lessons, and
even spoke to their mother about their childish
difficulties, stopping her, perhaps, when she was just
on the point of solving a difficult problem, by asking
some simple question, such as what seven times seven
made. Yet, so long as the children worked well, the
mother never became impatient, but was always

ready to stop and tell them kindly and gently what they wanted to know, and then go back to her work.

This power which Mrs. Somerville possessed of working without being disturbed by what was going on around her was all the more remarkable because of the abstruse character of her work. For a long time astronomers had had a theory that ages and ages ago the whole solar system was composed of a sort of nebulous gas, and that the planets were simply portions of this gas which had shot off, as it were, and were now revolving round the largest portion— the sun.

Laplace's work in astronomy had been to prove that this theory was true; he had worked it out by algebra in a way which no one could disprove. Yet, as he had written only for people who understood the subject, he had not troubled to simplify matters at all, and had not given any diagrams or figures. In trying to give the unlearned an idea of the theory, Mrs. Somerville had to work out his problems over again, and explain clearly subjects which in themselves were not at all clear. That she could do this, and at the same time teach little girls grammar and arithmetic, is almost incredible.

A very amusing instance of her marvellous power of withdrawing herself from the outside world whilst working is given by one of the little girls in question. One day when Mrs. Somerville was living in Rome, she went to hear a celebrated poetess declaim some

of her own poetry. For a while she listened atten-
tively, and then, perhaps, not finding the declamation
very interesting, she began to think of her own
writing, and became so entirely absorbed in her
thoughts, that though still having the appearance of
a listener, she in reality heard not a word that was
spoken. This was, in truth, a good thing for her,
because she had a great dislike to flattery, and it
happened that the poetess, quite unexpectedly, left
other subjects, and occupied herself in most enthusiastic praise of her talented hearer. Yet Mrs. Somerville sat through it all quite calm and unmoved, never
changing countenance at all. Her friends were amazed
at her serenity ; but when the performance was over
they were much amused to discover that she had,
during the whole time, been thinking her own thoughts,
and was quite unaware of what was going on.

Mrs. Somerville was about three years writing her
" Mechanism of the Heavens," which was the title
given to her account of Laplace's great book.

At last it was finished, and the manuscript sent
off to Lord Brougham, in order that he might decide,
as previously arranged, whether it should be torn up
or not. But the book was not destined to be at once
destroyed. On the contrary, it was published, and
· was very highly praised by all who read it. It at
once brought great honour to its author, and clever
men wrote from all quarters to congratulate her
on her success. The great astronomer, Sir John

Herschel, Dr. Whewell, afterwards Master of Trinity College, Cambridge, and Professor Peacock, a great mathematician, were amongst the number of those who praised the book. Added to this, Mrs. Somerville was elected an honorary member of the Royal Astronomical Society, of the Royal Academy at Dublin, and of the Société de Physique et d'Histoire Naturelle of Geneva; her bust was ordered to be placed in the great hall of the Royal Society, and a literary pension of £300 a year was bestowed upon her. Some years later she was made a member of the Royal Italian Geographical Society, and the first gold medal ever awarded by the society was voted by acclamation to her. Her work had been hard, but the recognition came very speedily. She was fêted and complimented wherever she went, and at once took up her position as one of the scientific leaders of the day.

One of the honours bestowed upon this gifted woman was so extraordinary that it deserves special mention. About this time all Englishmen were thrown into a state of great excitement and interest because the ships which had gone in quest of a north-west passage from the Atlantic to the Pacific had returned home.

Mrs. Somerville was gratified to be told that an island so far to the north that it was all but perpetually covered with ice and snow had been named "Somerville," after herself. It would, however, be a mistake to conclude that this had been done because Mrs. Somerville had distinguished herself in mathematics. The real reason why she had been thus celebrated was that, having been invited to inspect the ships preparing for one of these expeditions, she had put in practice her knowledge of cookery by making a large quantity of orange marmalade, and presenting it to the officers for use during the voyage. It is easy to understand that the appreciation of the marmalade would cause her name to be remembered with gratitude when her mathematical capacity had ceased to interest.

Another unusual compliment paid to her was that a well-known ship builder named after her a fine vessel which was intended for the China and India trade, and obtained through a mutual friend a copy of her bust for the figure-head. Unfortunately, the *Mary Somerville* was lost in her first voyage. It was supposed that she had foundered during a typhoon in the China Sea.

When one has worked earnestly and long, it is very pleasant to have the value of the work appreciated. The sincere praise of our fellows cannot but be agreeable to those who know that they have deserved it. Also, there is no denying that when one has been ridiculed and sneered at for pursuing a certain career, and then it turns out that the said career leads to usefulness and glory, it is a little gratifying to hear the sneerers and grumblers joining in the

D

general hurrahs. But to an affectionate, true-hearted woman like Mrs. Somerville, no praise is so sweet as that which comes from those near and dear, and no hurrahs make such music as theirs. We are not astonished, therefore, to find the following entry in Mrs. Somerville's " Recollections " :—

"Our relations and others who had so severely criticised and ridiculed me, astonished at my success, were now loud in my praise. But the warmth with which Somerville entered into my success deeply affected me. Not one in ten thousand would have rejoiced at it as he did. But he was of a generous nature, far above jealousy, and he continued through life to take the kindest interest in all I did."

By way of taking a rest after her achievements, Mrs. Somerville soon after this went with her family to stay on the Continent for awhile. Wherever she went, scientific men received her with enthusiasm. If she had been so inclined, she might now have given herself up to enjoyment, feeling that she had done what it had been possible for no other woman to do. But the hunger for work and for increased knowledge, so far from being satisfied, was only slightly appeased, and in a very short time this indefatigable worker was busy once more—it seemed as if she could not stop. True, she went into society a great deal ; she made the acquaintance of princes, ambassadors, professors, and celebrated people of all sorts; and in her genial, witty way she noted their peculiarities and enjoyed their company. But she never gave up her work; she still economised her time, and made the most of every opportunity ; and though she could not rise early, as she formerly did (for her application had told upon her health, and she was so delicate that she had to lie in bed till mid-day), she did not waste time on that account, but made a practice of writing while in bed.

The result of all this industry soon appeared. Some time after the publication of her first work, Mrs. Somerville brought out a second volume, almost as profound as the first, and quite original. It was called " The Connection of the Physical Sciences," and then, in course of time, a third volume appeared on " Physical Geography." The last-named of these is the one by which its author is best known.

Soon after his wife had begun to work on " Physical Geography," Dr. Somerville's health failed, and the family took up their residence in Italy ; they went from one city to another, meeting kind friends and warm admirers everywhere, and thoroughly enjoying the beautiful scenery and social life of the country. As was usual with them, they became intimate with the " best people " wherever they pitched their tent, so that the life of the great writer is to a large extent made up of the story of the people whom she knew. She had eyes to see and a mind to understand all that was going on around her, and so she missed nothing. The after-part of every day she gave up to amusement

D 2

and to excursions to picture galleries and antiquities, but the whole of her mornings she gave to work. This rule she laid down inflexibly, and when possible, allowed nothing to interfere with her resolution. So success once more crowned her efforts. Though the "Physical Geography" was a most advanced work, full of thought and research, requiring many years of study, it was at length completed, and was a marvel to all who read it. Whatever else Mrs. Somerville had accomplished, she had proved that women were capable of scientific thought.

Mrs. Somerville was sixty-eight years of age when her "Physical Geography" was published ; and persons less energetic than herself would have thought that having done so much, the time had come when she might rest and be thankful. But she found no pleasure in idleness. Still she visited her numerous friends, making fresh acquaintance continually amongst the learned and talented ; still she travelled from place to place, seeing much that was wonderful and beautiful, and rejoicing in all things fair ; and still she took an eager interest in the political events of the day. Living, as she did, for the most part in Italy, she was naturally much occupied with the stirring events which were then occurring. Her sympathies had always been with liberal opinions, and long before Italy was united under Victor Emmanuel, she believed that its unity would be brought about. When it was accomplished, she was enthusiastically glad.

Mrs. Somerville's love of animals was one of her chief characteristics. When quite a girl she went on one occasion with her father on a tour in the Highlands. On her return she found that a pet goldfinch which had been left in the charge of the servants, and neglected by them, had died of starvation. She was almost heart-broken at the event, and in writing her "Recollections," seventy years after, she mentioned it, and said that as she wrote she felt deep pain. After her second marriage, and a little while before she wrote her first book, she tells how she "liked" a certain individual, on account of his kindness to animals. She even believed to some extent in the immortality of animals, on the ground that if animals have no future, and as the existence of many is most wretched, it would seem as if some were created for uncompensated misery, which would be contrary to the attributes of God's mercy and justice. She was very energetic in trying to get a law passed in the Italian Parliament for the protection of animals. In writing on this subject, she said : " We English cannot boast of humanity so long as our sportsmen find pleasure in shooting down tame pigeons as they fly terrified out of a cage."

Of another acquaintance she says : " He was one of the most amiable men I ever met with, and quite won my heart one day at table, when they were talking of the number of singing birds that were eaten in Italy—nightingales, goldfinches, and robins—

he called out, "What! robins! our household birds! I would as soon eat a child!"

One of the subjects in which Mrs. Somerville was particularly interested was what is called the "Emancipation of Women." She had herself in early life known what it was to face the prejudice which was a few years ago very common in Great Britain against literary and scientific education for women, but she lived to see a great change in public opinion on this point. As she grew older she became quite zealous in doing what she could to encourage women to cultivate their minds. She rejoiced exceedingly when Girton College was founded, and said that it was a great step in the true direction. She was also very wishful that women should take an interest in politics and headed one petition, and frequently signed others, to Parliament for Female Suffrage. She was also a member of the London General Committee for Woman Suffrage. Yet she by no means sympathised with the fear that if women were to receive a solid education, they would in consequence lose their feminine grace and would leave their domestic duties unperformed. Indeed, she was a bright example to the contrary. It has been already told that she was a good cook, a good needlewoman, a famous housewife, a good wife and mother. And she had also an abundant store of common sense.

Miss Edgeworth said of her, "While her head is among the stars, her feet are firm upon the earth."

With her "smiling eyes and pink colour, her soft voice, strong well-bred Scottish accent, and natural modesty," she must have been a most charming individual—as different as possible from the ogress which she would have been if the pictures of advanced women drawn by those who oppose her opinions were always true.

The last years of this great woman were spent in Italy. They were very calm and peaceful.

When eighty years of age she lost her husband; and after what has been said of the sympathy, love, and confidence which existed between them, it can be imagined that this was a most grievous sorrow. Five years later Woronzow Greig, the son to whom she was so warmly attached, died, and this event robbed her of one of her greatest delights. Yet she bore it with calm courage. Indeed, in reading her " Recollections " we receive the impression that the inevitable partings with her friends were cheered by the thought that the separation was only for a short time. As she was so old, she would soon join the loved ones. She thought of death and eternity with the most perfect composure and confidence in the mercy of God; and her belief in immortality was so firm and decided that she even allowed herself to hope that she would meet in the future state the animals she had loved. Whatever our opinion may be as to her ground for this hope, it is certain that to her it was a great comfort.

When eighty-nine years of age, Mrs. Somerville published yet another work, "Molecular and Microscopic Science," which was an account of some of the most recent researches of modern science. This book seems to have been begun and continued, as much as anything, because the author, after her husband's death, wanted something to do to occupy her mind. Her daughters urged her to begin it, although in order to carry out her purpose she had to make many experiments, examine different objects through the microscope, and read difficult scientific periodicals and treatises; and all this for an old lady of eighty-nine, who "was very deaf and had shaking hands, and got sooner tired when writing than she used to do," was no trifling business. But Mrs. Somerville commenced work with her accustomed energy, though "she did not hurry, nor did she see the need of it."

She wrote regularly every morning before rising, from eight till twelve or one o'clock, and as she wrote "a mountain sparrow, a great pet, used to perch on her arm." For eight years this little bird was her constant companion, and used to sleep upon her arm while she was writing. It came to a violent end, for it was drowned in the water-jug, to the great grief of its famous mistress. After losing this bird, she made a pet of a beautiful long-tailed parroquet, who was her constant companion, and very familiar.

This last book must have cost Mrs. Somerville a great effort. During its course she had a severe illness, which tried her greatly. Before it was completed her son died. But she persevered with it, and it remains a monument of her untiring industry and energy. Yet in speaking of it afterwards, she said : " In writing this book I made a great mistake, and repent it. Mathematics are the natural bent of my mind ; if I had devoted myself exclusively to that study, I might probably have written something useful."

Indeed she knew her own powers well ; her bent was decidedly for mathematics. Only a short time before her death, when in her ninety-second year, she wrote : " My memory of ordinary events, and especially of the names of people, is failing, but not for mathematical and scientific subjects. I am still able to read books on the higher algebra for four or five hours in the morning, and even to solve the problems. Sometimes I find them difficult, but my old obstinacy remains, for if I do not succeed to-day, I attack them again on the morrow."

Again she wrote : " Though far advanced in years, I take as lively an interest as ever in passing events. I regret that I shall not live to know the result of the expedition to determine the currents of the ocean, the distance of the earth from the sun, determined by the transits of Venus, and the source of the most renowned of rivers, the discovery of which will immortalise the name of Dr. Livingstone." And in another place : " I must mention how mucn I was pleased to hear that

Mr. Herbert, M.P., has brought in a bill to protect land birds, which has been passed in Parliament; but I am grieved to find that 'the lark, which at heaven's gate sings,' is thought unworthy of man's protection. Among the numerous plans for the education of the young, let us hope that mercy may be taught as a part of religion."

Thus interested and occupied, the last weeks of life passed peacefully away, with higher algebra in the morning, Shakespeare, Dante, and more modern light reading, besides the newspapers, the visits of friends, cheerful conversation, and needlework, during the rest of the day.

Mrs. Somerville's old age was a thoroughly happy one. She had always had a great dread of outliving her intellect, but this trial was spared her. Although she attained so great an age, she was healthy in body and vigorous in mind to the last. With the one exception of deafness, she had none of the infirmities of age. She could read small print with ease and without glasses, even by lamp-light, and when very old, resumed the habit of working with her needle, being very much gratified to find that she could "count the threads of a fine canvas without spectacles." She understood and worked out difficult problems with the same quickness and ease which she displayed when young. Her last occupations, continued to the actual day of her death, were the revision and completion of a treatise, written years before, on the "Theory of Differences," and the study of a book on Quaternions.

During her last days this talented woman often said that "not even in the joyous spring of life had she been more truly happy." To quote her daughter's touching words: "Her affection for those she loved, and her sympathy for all living beings, remained to the last as fervent as ever; nor did her ardent desire for and belief in the ultimate religious and moral improvement of mankind diminish. . . . God was indeed loving and merciful to her; not only did He allow her to retain her faculties unimpaired to so great an age, but the weary trial of long-continued illness was spared her."

She died in sleep, on the morning of the 29th November, 1872. For her, Death lost its terrors; her pure spirit passed away so gently that those around her scarcely perceived when she left them. "It was the beautiful and painless close of a beautiful and a happy life."

Shortly after her death a movement was started to commemorate her name. This resulted in the establishment of the Somerville Hall at Oxford, and a "Mary Somerville" scholarship of £30 a year for three years awarded for mathematics. Somerville Hall was opened in 1879; it has succeeded so well, that twice since then it has been found necessary to enlarge it. At the present time there are in connection with it, besides the "Mary Somerville" scholarship, one scholarship of £60 for three years, and one of £40 for three years. It is hoped that very shortly the council will be able to offer three additional scholarships of £20 a year each. The life of the students is modelled on that of an English family ; and care is taken in the conduct of the institution that members of different religious denominations shall be placed on the same footing. Thus it will be seen that in honour of Mary Somerville efforts are being made to promote a cause which lay very near her heart—namely, the higher education of women. Of the capacity of women to profit by this higher education, her own life was a signal proof.

(Our Portrait of Mrs. Somerville is taken, by permission, from a Bust at Girton College, Cambridge.)

MARY CARPENTER.

ONE day, at the beginning of this century, a clever and good man took his two little daughters, Mary and Anna, for a walk in the country, and led them into a field of new-mown hay. Anna rolled in the sunshine, and was happy, but this was not enough for four-year-old Mary, who saw the haymakers busily at work.

"I want to be ooseful; I want to be ooseful!" she cried, and she would not be content until her father cut a stick from the hedge, so that she might rake together the hay her sister scattered.

This little girl who "wanted to be ooseful" was Mary Carpenter, the woman who did more perhaps than any one else to lift destitute and criminal children out of their misery and sin. This pretty anecdote of her early childhood is told by her nephew Professor J. Estlin Carpenter, in the memoir he has written called "The Life and Work of Mary Carpenter."

Mary Carpenter was one of the World's Workers. Her field of work was very different from that of Mary Somerville, for Mary Somerville gave her mind to science, while Mary Carpenter gave her life and strength to trying to rescue the poor and degraded.

Mary Carpenter was born at Exeter on the 3rd of April, 1807. Her father was Dr. Lant Carpenter, a Unitarian minister, well known in his day for his ability, his enthusiastic philanthropy, and his simple, earnest piety. Mary had the greatest reverence for her father, and in many respects she was like him ; she inherited from him her industry, her warm sympathy with the miserable and suffering, and her deep religious feeling.

Mary's home was a very happy one, cheerful, frugal, and well ordered. The various members of the family loved each other very much ; they were all busy, and all in earnest. As the children grew up they were accustomed to find their father and mother interested in books and public questions ; they were well acquainted with the best poetry too, and the children quite early became familiar with it.

As a baby, Mary must have been rather precocious, and unlike other small children of her age. When about two years old she insisted on being called " Dr. Carpenter" in the nursery. Unlike Mrs. Somerville, she was very fond of dolls, and though much interested in lessons, was always content to turn away from them to look after the "grand affairs" of her waxen playthings.

When Mary was ten years old the family removed to Bristol, and Dr. Carpenter opened a school for about twelve boys. Amongst these pupils Mary very soon took her place, and was educated in subjects which were not often taught to girls at that time. She studied Latin, Greek and mathematics, geology, natural philosophy, and chemistry, and proved herself remarkably quick in learning. Dr. Martineau, in describing her at this time, says that as " a sedate little girl of twelve she looked at you so steadily, and always spoke like a book, so that in talking to her what you meant for sense seemed to turn into nonsense on the way. . . . She appeared to have the world, and all that had happened in it, at her fingers' ends, as if she had been always and everywhere in it."

When Mary was about twelve years old she was attacked by a very painful affection of the eyes. Her medical adviser was afraid that if great care was not taken she might become blind, and he ordered her to be kept for many weeks in a darkened room. An ordeal of this sort would be a great trial to any one, but it was particularly so to a child like Mary, fond of reading, and quite unaccustomed to waste her time. It would have been no wonder if she had been irritable and unreasonable under the trial, but she was nothing of the sort. She was sweet and patient through everything, and by way of still being a help in the household, she appointed herself timekeeper for the family, reminding the rest of their various engagements. During this imprisonment, as it may be called, Mary's sister Anna was very kind to her. She sat with her, read to her, and did what she could to make the time pass pleasantly. In later life this same sister Anna was her friend and companion in all her work.

Twice during her childhood Mary suffered from this affection of the eyes, and was compelled, on account of it, to give up work. This was all the more remarkable, because, as a woman, Mary's eyes were her most attractive feature. They were large and grey, and so expressive of earnestness and kindly penetration, that they exercised a sort of fascination over those who looked into them.

It is a very good thing when childhood is free from care. Young people who belong to happy homes usually go on from day to day having all that they need provided for them, and thinking perhaps that thus it will always be. But sooner or later there comes to all a reminder that they have their own work to do, and must take their share of the burden of life. Sometimes this reminder comes in the form of the death of a parent on whom they were accustomed to lean, sometimes in the failure of strength, sometimes it comes gently and gradually, sometimes suddenly and unexpectedly. Happy they who, whenever it comes, and however it comes, are prepared for action, and find themselves possessed of the tools they need.

To Mary Carpenter this reminder came when she was about seventeen years old. Then she realised that her father—her dear and honoured father—was working beyond his strength. He was a very busy man ; he had his church to look after, the school to superintend, literary work and philanthropic work devolving upon him, his family dependent on him, and his health began to fail. A weak girl under these circumstances would have been unhappy, and done nothing. She would have waited to see what came, and hoped that things would mend. But Mary was not weak; she was very strong. At once she prepared to rush to her father's rescue.

It would be a mistake to say that Mary *began* now to take upon herself a share of the burden of the family, for she had begun to do that long before. When she was quite a young girl she used to take her father's place in the school during his occasional absence from illness, and, with the assistance of her schoolfellow, the friend who afterwards became Dr. James Martineau, she superintended the lessons of the other pupils. She was so useful in the home, too, that when she had to go away her mother missed her help sadly. But more was wanted from her now. She saw that what was required was that her father should be relieved from the school altogether, and should have an easier life. Very steadily she set to work to accomplish this. She missed no opportunity of gaining knowledge, so that she might be fit to teach, and she took entire charge of the younger pupils. Not content with this, she resolved, after a time, to leave home and go out as a governess. She

E

found absence from home a trial, but on the whole her scheme was a success. It gave her courage and independence, and made her stronger for the work which was before her.

In the spring of 1829 Dr. Carpenter, finding that he did not recover his wonted health, determined to give up the school, and in its place it was decided that Mary, with her mother and sister, should commence a school for young ladies. This school was continued for sixteen years, and was fairly successful. The work was hard, but the workers felt that they were toiling for those they loved, and were being of use, and so they were content. In speaking of the work to a friend, Mary said, " School keeping is certainly difficult work, but we have so long been accustomed to have something to do, that I do not think we should be happy without some regular employment which is useful."

As was to be expected, Miss Carpenter was the mainstay of this new undertaking, and the girls under her charge looked upon her almost with awe as a sort of prodigy. They had reason to do so, for her attainments were very far in advance of those of ordinary women of her day. One of the school girls writing home, said, " Miss Carpenter is quite delightful. She understands Greek, Latin, Italian, French, and every other language, for anything I know to the contrary, for I only know of these through hearing her teach them. She is fond of poetry, conchology, and geology—the two last she seems to understand very well. In short, she seems to be universal."

While Miss Carpenter was thus busily occupied in teaching both living and dead languages, and scientific subjects on the week days, her time on Sundays was given to the Sunday school. From a very early age she had taken part in this work, and had always been very much interested in it. But in 1831 she was appointed superintendent of the school. It is scarcely necessary to say that she threw her whole heart into her task. She was not content with simply teaching her class on the Sunday. She made herself the friend of her scholars, inquired into their circumstances, followed them to their homes, introduced herself to their parents, and learnt all that she could about them. In this way she found out how miserable and poor many of them were, and, living as they did in such a degraded condition, how difficult it was for them to escape from sinking yet lower and lower.

Even in these days we sometimes think that people who differ in politics are very much more excited and bitter than they need be, and that if opponents would only discuss quietly and talk pleasantly together, they would respect each other more. What would the persons who think thus have said if they had watched events fifty or sixty years ago? At the very time that Miss Carpenter was made superintendent of the Sunday school, the country was in the greatest state of excitement. The House of

E 2

Lords had thrown out the great Reform Bill, and, as a consequence, the people were most impatient and angry. Large indignation meetings were held in different parts of the kingdom, and outrages and disturbances occurred every day.

In Bristol disorder was at its worst. The mob of Bristol was one of the fiercest in England. It happened that the Recorder of Bristol, Sir C. Wetherell, had been one of the most prominent anti-reformers, and that at this time it was his duty to visit Bristol to make the usual gaol delivery. The people of Bristol determined they would seize the opportunity to protest against his conduct in Parliament. Accordingly, when he entered the city, he was received with groans, yells, and hisses by the mob, his carriage was surrounded by an angry crowd, and when at last he managed to take his seat on the bench, the noise and confusion were so great that the court had to adjourn. The mob, finding themselves successful, became gradually more and more daring, and soon gained the upper hand. They made a rush on the police, and completely routed them. Troops were called in, but the rioters received them with showers of stones, bottles, and bricks, and several lives were lost.

At last they began to set public buildings and private dwellings on fire. They went about their work of destruction in a most systematic way, giving the inmates of each house half an hour's notice before setting it in flames. Then the leaders entered with turpentine and brushes, and smeared turpentine around to make the place burn more fiercely. With their axes also they cut holes in the floors of the burning houses, so that the air might enter and fan the fire. The consequence was, the flames burnt so fiercely that in some instances the rioters themselves were unable to escape, and perished with the burning buildings.

Miss Carpenter was one of those who had to look on powerless while Bristol was in flames. She knew—none better—how miserable and ignorant the people were who had done this thing ; how they were animated by hatred of the classes above them, feeling that they were wronged, though they could not have said how. She knew, too, that to a degree the hatred was justified, and that it was the cruelty and injustice of society which were driving these dangerous ones to crime. The Bristol riots broke out on the last Sunday in October. Mary Carpenter's biographer tells us that "the contrast between the peaceful sunshine of the autumn morning and the dreadful glare of the fire-lit sky at night fixed itself ineffaceably in her remembrance ; and her heart was filled with a deep pity for those whose mad passions had brought on the innocent such calamity and disgrace. The impression deepened as day after day brought tidings of fresh crime and misery. She began to ponder on the causes of the outbreak, and to find their place in the general circumstances of the time, and the desire was already stirring within her to devote herself to the service of the degraded around her."

After pondering thus for two months, Mary Carpenter made a solemn resolve to devote her life to trying to do good to others, caring not at all for her own comfort or labour. She even wrote down a sort of formal dedication of herself to the service of humanity, so that the written words might be a witness against herself if she failed to live up to them and deserted the sacred cause. But her purpose was too earnest, and her enthusiasm too deep to be forgotten. When the opportunity for action came she was ready, and the story of her life is the story of a brave woman, who accomplished wonders in saving the neglected and the miserable.

About this time Mary Carpenter made the acquaintance of two people who were destined to have a great influence over her life. One of these was the celebrated Rajah Rammohun Roy, and the other, Dr. Joseph Tuckerman, of Boston, America. Rammohun Roy it was who first made her think of helping the people of India, a work which for many years she was obliged to dismiss from her mind, but the desire for which formed now was cherished for more than thirty years, and was ultimately taken up. Dr. Tuckerman showed her that there was work to be done at home, in the streets and alleys which were within a stone's throw of her own dwelling. Both were earnest, brave, and good men.

Rammohun Roy was a young Brahman of high caste. He was exceedingly intelligent, highly educated, and very thoughtful. At a very early age he began to have doubts about the truth of the religion in which he had been brought up. As he spoke out what he thought very plainly and boldly, his father and friends were very angry with him. His mother, it is said, agreed with him, and was convinced by his arguments, but she refused to give up the religion of her friends and country. One day, when she was about to set out on a pilgrimage to Juggernaut, he remonstrated with her, and she said, "You are right, but I am a woman, and cannot give up observances which are a comfort to me." The son, however, did not shrink from giving up what he had ceased to believe in. He braved both the scorn of his acquaintances and the anger of his father, in order to be true to his convictions.

He continued his studies, went on to examine other religions, and found that they were all very much alike. At last his attention was directed to Christianity, and by it he was strongly attracted. He was particularly impressed by the precepts and life of Jesus, and although he never believed in the divinity of Christ, or agreed in opinion with orthodox English Christians, he freely declared that the precepts of Jesus led to peace and happiness.

When Rammohun Roy visited England he was warmly received wherever he went. At the time of his visit the Reform struggle was at its fiercest, and he took the greatest interest in the events of the time. He became acquainted with Dr. Carpenter, and was introduced by him to his family. Mary was delighted with him. She listened eagerly to all that he had to say about India, and especially about the condition of the women there, and she longed to go out and see whether it was not possible to do something to help them. Of course it was not possible. She had the school to attend to, and her parents needed her help ; but the idea was kept in reserve, and was acted on years after.

Rammohun Roy died a little more than two years after his arrival in England, when he was about fifty-three years of age. He overworked himself, and was attacked by a fever, which proved fatal. His death was a great shock to the friends who loved him, and who hoped he would have done great things for India. To no one was it a greater trouble than to Mary Carpenter. She mourned for him deeply, and the remembrance of his honesty and his earnestness remained to influence all her life.

Dr. Tuckerman was a very different man. He was an American, who for twenty-five years had been working amongst the poor, doing all he could to help them. His home was in Boston, and he had come to England for the benefit of his health. Like all good men of his kind, he had heard of Dr. Carpenter, and felt sure of sympathy from him and his friends. Very soon after his arrival in this country, therefore, he paid a visit to the Bristol home, and received a hearty welcome. He was invited to remain for awhile, and in this way he became intimate with Mary and the rest of the family. We can understand how eagerly the earnest-hearted woman, filled with pity and love for the poor, would listen to the story of the work which the earnest-hearted man had been able to accomplish ; how she would try to learn his methods, and long to imitate his example. Ill as he was, Dr. Tuckerman could not refrain from exploring the narrow streets and miserable alleys where the "dangerous classes " lived. We are not surprised to be told that in these excursions Mary was his companion.

One day, as Mary was walking with her guest through some of the streets which surrounded her father's chapel in " Lewin's Mead," a miserable, ragged boy darted out of a dark court and rushed wildly across their path. " That child," said Dr. Tuckerman, " should be followed to his home and seen after." Nothing more was said, but the remark was like the seed which fell into good ground, and brought forth fruit a hundred-fold. Thirty-six years after Mary repeated these words, and said that the moment of her hearing them was one of the quickening moments of her life. " His words," she said, " sank into my mind with a painful feeling that a duty was being neglected."

The sensitive girl told her sisters what had

happened, and together they resolved to see what could
be done. These girls were all busy. They had the
school to keep up, their brothers to educate, their
parents to care for, the charge of the family rested
upon them. Some would have said that with these
claims upon their time and strength, they were to be
excused if they left the wretched arabs and street
vagrants to get on as best they might. But Mary and
her sisters could not quieten their consciences thus.
They had been brought up from childhood to con-
sider the poor, and they were miserable when they
thought of the misery of others. So they called
their friends and neighbours together, and held a
consultation, and the result was that a Working
and Visiting Society was established, whose members
were to make it their duty to visit the poor, and
inquire into their actual condition, with the object of
relieving them. Of this society Mary Carpenter
was chosen secretary, and she occupied the post for
twenty years.

It is now about half a century since the Lewin's
Mead Working and Visiting Society was formed, and
it is very interesting to look back and note the
methods of work which these friends of the poor
adopted. District visiting was not then as usual as
it is now ; it was new and untried. Undertaken as it
was by earnest enthusiasts, who were unaccustomed
to the task, it would not have been at all astonishing
if the visitors had commenced with the notion of

relieving instantly the poverty with which they came
into contact ; bestowing freely indiscriminate gifts of
money and clothing upon those who stood sorely in
need of both. Inexperienced workers among the
poor almost always make this mistake. They give
to all who tell a pitiful tale, and the more squalid the
surroundings the more liberal is the relief bestowed.
The consequence is that the poor and idle give up
altogether trying to mend matters, and concern themselves with appearing as needy as possible. The poor
and industrious meanwhile, who struggle to make the
best of things, are left unaided. What is wanted is
that industry and thrift should be encouraged, idleness and extravagance discountenanced, that so independence and self-respect may grow and increase.
Mary Carpenter and her fellow-workers understood
this well.

Bristol was at this time one of the worst cities in
the kingdom for the poverty and distress of its lowest
classes. Its narrow courts reeked with filth, and
scenes inexpressibly painful were to be witnessed
there. It was not easy for ladies, who lived in well-
ordered homes, who had refined tastes and loved
intellectual pursuits, to plunge into the midst of these
horrors, to breathe the foul air, and come into contact
with low ideas and vicious life. But Mary Carpenter,
having once put her hand to the plough, never turned
back. She loved books, poetry, and science as much
as any one could do, but she cheerfully left them all

to help those who needed her help. It is said that when the time came for apportioning the different districts to the various visitors, Mary always chose for herself the poorest and the worst. Sometimes the dirt, squalor, and sin she saw were so dreadful, that she was utterly disgusted and filled with loathing ; but love and pity invariably triumphed in her heart, and made her willing to endure pain, if only she might be of service to these poor lost ones.

In the midst of all this work, Mary Carpenter did not entirely give up her studies. Poetry, science, and art afforded her great pleasure, and reading was her great resource. It is interesting to note that even at this early period Mary Carpenter was particularly fond of Wordsworth's poems. Fifty years ago Wordsworth was not esteemed so highly as he is now ; the people of his own day were sometimes inclined to speak of him with scorn. But with Mary Carpenter he was a special favourite. She had the wit to discover his merit quite early, and she felt kindly disposed to people when once she knew that they loved Wordsworth. Turner's pictures, too, she highly appreciated after a while, though not at first. Very often when she was in London, and felt tired out, she used to steal away to the National Gallery, sit before one of Turner's great pictures for a time, and come away refreshed. Mary Carpenter had a great love for art.

In the year 1840 came the great sorrow of Mary

Carpenter's life—the death of her father. Dr. Carpenter had been delicate for a long time, so it was decided that he should go abroad for the benefit of his health ; and while away from home he was accidentally drowned. He had been so good, so wise, tender, and clever, that he was almost revered by his family, and his removal was a bitter stroke.

Mary had a most profound affection for her father. There had always been a sweet confidence between them ; they had understood each other, and trusted each other, and when this dearly-loved father was taken away, it seemed to Mary Carpenter as if "the sun had gone out of her sky." But she could not give way to her sorrow. Her mother had to be comforted, the family life had to be kept up, and in this Christian home all were ready to sacrifice themselves for the sake of the others. Friends outside sympathised and condoled, and Mary felt very grateful to them all. She knew that her father's life's work had been nobly done ; she looked forward to meeting him again in a land where parting will be no more. And so, although it was a long time before she could recover her brightness of spirit, she at least became calm, and while still cherishing her love for her father, she was able to resign herself to the will of God. In short, Mary Carpenter saw clearly what thousands have seen before her, and what thousands will yet be brought to see—that death is by no means the greatest evil. Sin is infinitely worse. We can endure to be separated by death from those we love, when we can remember that while here they were faithful and earnest workers for what is true and right. The unendurable pain comes when they have given cause for regret.

Within a few years after the death of her father, Mary Carpenter's revered friend, Dr. Tuckerman, died. This was an additional sorrow. Mary had the greatest veneration for this excellent man. To use her own language, "for six years he was a guide and rest to her soul." Thirty-five years afterwards, when a scheme which lay very near her heart—that of the establishment of feeding industrial schools — was successfully floated, she regarded it as a carrying out of Dr. Tuckerman's idea.

In May, 1843, about three years after the death of her father, Mary Carpenter formally "took the pledge," and became a teetotaller. The event ought to be noticed, because the lady herself thought so much of it. She always insisted with ardour on the importance of workers among the poor being total abstainers, and once said that "teetotalism, divested of the nonsense and vulgarity which too often accompany it, appeared to her to be the sublimest institution that exists next to Christianity." Once, when writing to a friend, she said :—"The slaves here for whom I am most concerned, are those enslaved to the use of intoxicating liquors. I feel on this subject somewhat as you do about slavery, and perhaps in some respects more painfully, as here the soul is enslaved as well as the body, and the whole family is ruined by the vice of one. No one who has not come into immediate contact, as I have, with such cases, can realise the horror of them ; indeed, I am fully persuaded that no legislation can raise the working classes of England as long as this evil exists among them."

When Mary Carpenter was superintendent of the Sunday school she was very anxious to awaken the curiosity and intelligence of the scholars, and in order to do this she arranged a museum of geological specimens and natural objects, which she presented to the school, and which she was delighted to show to the children when they were willing to look. She still visited the poor in their own homes too, and sympathised with them in their trouble ; and as she gradually came to know them well, she felt more than ever convinced that there was a possibility that very much might be done to raise them.

The poor and destitute who attended the Sunday schools, however, were what were called " occasional criminals," that is, they now and again transgressed against the law of the land, and were brought up before the magistrates. But below these there was another class, who were called the " habitual criminals," who were no sooner released from prison for one offence than they committed another, and who had no idea of being industrious and working for their own living. For these people gaols and penitentiaries were no good, and free day schools they refused to attend. There were no School Board schools at that time into which vagrant children could be compelled to go, and the consequence was that juvenile crime was increasing very rapidly, and there seemed no hope that the evil would ever be lessened; for it was a painful truth that the numbers of the "habitual criminals" were continually being added to from the ranks of the "occasional criminals," and things were rapidly going from bad to worse.

It was a blessing for England and for the world, that at this point a good woman stepped forward and said that things should not be allowed to go on as they were; but that an earnest attempt should be made to rescue these hapless little ones from the depths of degradation which seemed to be their fate. This good woman was Mary Carpenter.

Of course Miss Carpenter was not alone in what she did; she found friends to sympathise with her and help her. Workers for God are seldom left quite solitary. Even at the darkest times they discover, like Elijah, that there are others as well as themselves "who have not bowed the knee to Baal." So it was with Mary Carpenter. Good men and women besides herself were willing to work for the children on both sides of the Atlantic. There were the Rev. John Clay, of Preston; the Rev. T. Carter, of Liverpool; the Rev. Sydney Turner, of Red Hill; Sheriff Watson, of Aberdeen; the Rev. W. C. Osborn; Mr. Russell Scott, of Bath; Lord Ashley, who afterwards became Lord Shaftesbury, and last but not least, Mr. Matthew Davenport Hill, the Recorder of Birmingham, with many others. With all these Mary Carpenter was at one.

But of all her friends there was not one with whom Mary Carpenter was more heartily in sympathy than with Mr. Matthew Davenport Hill. This good man had filled the office of Recorder of Birmingham. In this capacity he had had much to do with young criminals, and had come to the opinion that imprisonment in gaol was worse than useless for them, because it too often brought them into companionship with those more hardened than themselves. Again and again Mr. Davenport Hill had tried to convince the public of the necessity for reformatories, and the importance of education for the prevention and cure of crime. But for a long time he spoke in vain. What he and his friends would have liked would have been the establishment of schools like our present Board Schools, which children should be compelled to attend. But that was a great step in advance, and the public were not yet prepared to go so far. For the destitute and criminal he urged the establishment of reformatories and ragged schools.

The one fact which led people like Miss Carpenter and Mr. Matthew Davenport Hill to desire the education of the masses, was the prevalence of juvenile

F

crime. A quarter of a century after Mary Carpenter's
first ragged school was opened, Mr. Forster's Education Act became law, and the attendance of children
at school was made compulsory. The beneficial
effect of that Act, and of the efforts of philanthropists
to improve the condition of the poor, has since been
proved. It is very remarkable that when Miss
Davenport Hill (the daughter of Mr. Davenport Hill,
Mary Carpenter's friend) was seeking re-election as a
member of the School Board for London, she drew
attention to the fact that within twenty years juvenile
crime had diminished by more than half. In 1870
seven out of every hundred habitual criminals were
under sixteen. In 1884 there were only three out of
every hundred, and these were almost all children
who had managed to escape being sent to school.
Thus the daughter was permitted to rejoice in a good
work that her father had done much to bring about.

Years before this a friend from New York, the
Rev. Dr. Dewey, in talking about juvenile delinquents
with Mary Carpenter, had said very emphatically,
" *Do something!* " These words sank into her heart,
and she never rested until she had begun to "do"
something. As early as 1846 she had, in conjunction
with a few friends, made a determined plunge, and
opened a ragged school. This school was held in a
room in Lewin's Mead, a long street in which stood
Dr. Carpenter's chapel. Lewin's Mead was not a
very inviting spot, but it was exactly the place for

the purpose. Miss Cobbe tells us that on a winter's night, when half the gas lights were out, it consisted chiefly of dens of drink and infamy, before which groups of miserable, drunken men and women used to shout, scream, and fight. The ordinary Bristol policemen were never to be seen at night in Lewin's Mead ; it was said that they were afraid to show themselves in the place. A short time before the ragged school was opened, some Bow Street constables had been sent down to ferret out a crime which had been committed there, and they reported that there was not in all London such a nest of wickedness as existed there.

The children who attended the school were exactly of the class whom it was desirable to reach. It was literally a "ragged" school. None of the children had shoes and stockings, some had no shirt and no home, sleeping in casks on the quay, or on steps, and living by petty thefts. Professor Carpenter tells us that on the first Sunday after the school was opened about twenty boys were assembled, and some who came in the morning brought more in the afternoon, which showed that they liked it. But beginning to be tired in the afternoon one of them said, " Now let us fight," and in an instant they were all fighting. Peace was, however, soon restored, and the proceedings went on with greater order than could have been expected.

Fortunately, kind friends came forward with

F 2

money to assist the ragged school, and a master was found who had a special gift for dealing with the street arabs. A band of workers, too, offered to help in the work, and in a very short time the school was so great a success that even the police noticed what a difference it made in the neighbourhood.

This encouraged the managers, and they opened a night school in connection with the ragged school, and to this there flocked a crowd of young men and women, so degraded in character that even Mary Carpenter's strong spirit quailed. One Sunday evening no fewer than two hundred pupils attended the school, and these were so rough and unmanageable that when the time came for dismissing the school, and an attempt was made to conclude with prayer, a small riot broke out, and the court resounded with screams and blows. Working men offered their help, but it was of no avail, and for a time it was necessary to call in the police. A rather amusing anecdote is told about the member of the force who was summoned to assist on the occasion. He came and did what he could, but very speedily the master recovered his control, and there was nothing for the officer to do. "It was not long before he was one day reported to the magistrate for neglect of duty, having been two hours in the ragged school setting copies to the boys."

Miserable as was the district where the first Bristol ragged school was located, St. James's Back, the

filthy lane in which the second school was situated,
was more miserable still. It was, indeed, a regular
haunt of ragamuffins. Once more helped by her
friends, Miss Carpenter bought one or two old houses
in St. James's Back, and converted them into schools.
Day by day, week by week, month by month, she
was to be found at these schools, going through the
routine which so many enthusiasts are ready to take
up for a little while, but which they are even more
ready to relinquish when they discover that there is
very little excitement about it, but only a dull con-
flict with misery and ingratitude. Discouragement of
this kind never affected Mary Carpenter. No matter
what inducements she might have to go elsewhere,
two nights in every week found her regularly at the
schools, which were attended by the off-scouring of
the streets, and day after day found her in the same
place ready to take a class, to help in distributing
soup to the hungry, or to take upon herself the larger
part of the toil that had to be gone through.

Going regularly thus to the school, of course she
soon became familiar with the ways of the children,
and also with the people of the neighbourhood. She
never had any fear in traversing these wretched courts
and alleys, and would go alone, and at night, into
places where policemen only went by twos. To quote
the touching words of her biographer, "The street
quarrel was hushed at her approach, as a guilty lad
slunk away to avoid her look of sorrowful reproof;

and her approving word, with the gift of a flower, a picture, or a Testament, often made sad homes cheerful, and renewed the courage of the wavering."

It would be a mistake, however, to suppose that Miss Carpenter's influence was so powerful that her rough pupils at once became docile when she appeared, and that rudeness and lawlessness changed into gentleness and order in her presence. She had her encouragements, of course, even she could not have kept on without them ; but she had her trials too in full abundance. Miss Cobbe, in an article published some years ago in the *Modern Review*, has drawn a picture of Mary Carpenter while at work, which is wonderfully life-like and real. Miss Cobbe says :—

" It was a wonderful spectacle to see Mary Carpenter sitting patiently before the large school gallery in St. James's Back, teaching, singing, and praying with the wild street-boys, in spite of endless interruptions caused by such proceedings as shooting marbles at any object behind her, whistling, stamping, fighting, shrieking out "Amen," in the middle of the prayer, and sometimes rising *en masse*, and tearing like a troop of bisons in hob-nailed shoes down from the gallery, round the great school-room, and down the stairs, and into the street. These irrepressible outbreaks she bore with infinite good-humour."

In the course of her daily work Miss Carpenter must have had some strange experiences, and it is greatly to be regretted that the anecdotes which have come to us are so few and far between. Some little idea of her method of teaching we can gain from a journal of her school-work which she kept for some years. Here is a short extract :—"I showed my scholars the orrery, which greatly delighted them, and they seemed quite to understand it, and to enter into the idea of the inclination of the earth's axis producing a change of seasons. This class had never seen a map, and had the greatest difficulty in realising it. T. was delighted to see Bristol, Keynsham, and Bath. I always begin with the 'known;' carrying them on afterwards to the 'unknown.'

"I had taken to my class on the preceding week some specimens of ferns, neatly gummed on white paper; they were much struck with their beauty, but none knew what they were, though W. thought he had seen them growing; one thought they were palm trees. They seemed interested in the account of their fructification I gave them. This time I took a piece of coal-shale, with impressions of ferns, to show them. I explained that this had once been in a liquid state, telling them that some things could be proved to be certain, while others were doubtful ; that time did not permit me to explain the proofs to them, nor would they understand them if I did ; but that I was careful to tell them nothing as certain which could not be fully proved. I then told each to examine the specimen, and tell me what he thought it was. W.

gave so bright a smile that I saw he knew; none of
the others could tell; he said they were ferns, like
what I showed them last week, but he thought they
were chiselled on the stone. Their surprise and
pleasure were great when I explained the matter to
them.

"The history of Joseph : they all found a difficulty
in realising that this had actually occurred. One
asked if Egypt existed now, and if people lived in it.
When I told them that buildings now stood which
had been erected about the time of Joseph, one said
that it was impossible, as they must have fallen down
ere this. I showed them the form of a pyramid, and
they were satisfied. One asked if *all* books were
true.

"The story of Macbeth impressed them much.
They knew the name of Shakespeare, having seen his
name over a public house."

Miss Cobbe, too, tells of a boy who defined
conscience as "a thing a gentleman hasn't got, who,
when a boy finds his purse and gives it back to him,
doesn't give the boy sixpence."

Another boy who, sharing in a Sunday evening
lecture on "Thankfulness," and being asked what
pleasure he enjoyed most in the course of the year,
replied candidly, "Cock-fightin', ma'am ; there's a pit
up by the 'Black Boy' as is worth anythink in
Brissel."

Girls will perhaps be sorry to hear that Miss

Carpenter found much more satisfaction in teaching boys than girls. With the boys, she said, she found little or no difficulty. They were sure to be interested in the lessons ; their wits were active enough, though their ignorance of common every-day matters frequently amazed her. They were quick to receive the facts of natural history, and readily applied the principles underlying the incidents of history to their own circumstances. But the girls were most stolid, and they often listened to her teaching with a stupidity that almost made her desperate.

When teaching these poor children, Miss Carpenter was accustomed to pay special attention to the Scripture lessons. In every way that it was possible she tried to make her pupils understand the story of the life of Jesus, and never wearied of unfolding to them the beauties of the Gospel narrative. When first they attended the school they were so wild and unruly that there was scarcely one of them to whom she could venture to read the Bible, while numbers had never seen or heard of the book. But the teacher was not dismayed ; very patiently she set to work, first with very short lessons, which were afterwards extended as the pupils showed signs of interest. Pictures, also, and any curiosities that could be obtained, either from her own cabinets or the collections of her friends, were freely employed for illustration, and no pains were spared to rouse the interest of the class.

Some of the boys when they left the school returned to their old habits of begging and stealing, but there were others upon whom the lessons thus given were not thrown away, and Miss Carpenter was cheered again and again by discovering that the efforts which she and her friends had made had been rewarded by the rescue of these poor boys from a life of degradation and shame. One secret of her success was, that she always tried to keep her hold of the boys after they had left the schools. When it was possible she placed them in situations, and found them honest work to do, and in several instances she kept up a correspondence with those who had left the country, sending them illustrated papers and magazines as a token of her remembrance and continued interest in them.

In thus trying to keep a hold on the children Miss Carpenter was sometimes successful, but oftener she failed, so that at last she was convinced that to save the children of the perishing and dangerous classes ragged schools were not sufficient, because in ragged schools the children were only partially under the influence of the teachers, the greater part of their time was spent in their old haunts in the companionship of the degraded and vicious, whilst, worst of all, they could come to school or stay away as they were disposed.

This Miss Carpenter felt very strongly was a mistake. She maintained, that for the different

classes of poor children, the destitute, the homeless,
and the criminal, there ought to be different sorts of
schools ; good free day schools and industrial schools
for the former, and reformatory schools for the thieves
and vagabonds. These ideas she stated clearly in a
book which about this time she published, and which
was entitled " Reformatory Schools for the Children
of the Perishing and Dangerous Classes and for Juvenile Offenders."

Mary Carpenter would have been very unlike
herself if, seeing that a great evil existed, and feeling sure that something could be done to remedy it,
she had not at once set to work. True, she was
already fully occupied, not only in trying to rouse
public attention to the condition of juvenile criminals,
but also on her ragged school and night and day
school. The ragged school at this time, that is about
the year 1850, had just been enlarged. Bath-room
and wash-houses had been added to it, and one
portion of the squalid court in which it was situated
had been turned into a playground, where the boys
could play merrily without being exposed to the
temptations of the street. It is interesting to be told,
because it shows how Miss Carpenter would have
sympathised with some of the workers of to-day, that
in this playground creepers were trained against the
walls, and that the benevolent lady who had arranged
everything, used to watch the lads at their play, and
was pleased when she saw that they were careful not

to injure the plants. In the buildings adjoining the school, too, she had some rooms fitted up in which poor homeless boys could have a night's lodging on occasion.

The ragged schools, however, benefited only the poor and destitute ; and tuned as her ear was to the cry of the miserable, the air for her was vocal on all sides with the groan of the criminals.

At length, to her great joy, she saw the way open before her, and she resolved to act. The task which she now set herself was neither more nor less than the establishment in Bristol of a reformatory school where young thieves and law-breakers could be trained and disciplined into ways of righteousness. For a long time she had believed the change could be effected ; now she would actually try the experiment. If she could prove that to reform young offenders was possible, others might be willing to make a like trial.

The first thing was to find suitable premises for the new school. Mary Carpenter and the friends who worked with her were thoroughly convinced of the importance of their school being situated in the country. They believed that country occupations, such as working on a farm, attending to a garden, and looking after live stock, were specially likely to interest and benefit boys who had been brought up in the misery of a town life, and they were anxious too that these poor children should have an opportunity of understanding the wonders of Nature.

Fortunately the right spot was soon discovered. About four miles from Bristol there was a village called Kingswood, in which stood an empty building, which had been erected by John Wesley with the intention of using it as a school for the education of the sons of ministers. The property, which included a farm and farm buildings, as well as a school-house containing accommodation for about a hundred children, covered twelve acres ; so that in all ways it was admirably fitted for a "rural reformatory." Accordingly the decision to take it was made. Mr. Russell Scott, of Bath, furnished the money for the purchase, Lady Byron and other friends generously helped to furnish, and Kingswood Reformatory was opened.

Kingswood was opened early in September, 1852. The master and mistress were engaged, the premises were set in order, and all was ready. Mary Carpenter was delighted. In a letter to a friend her mother said, "It is quite a happiness to see Mary ; she is so cheerful, and interests herself so much more in her friends. Her desire is gratified, her soul finds repose, and her affections expand."

When we have aimed at something for a long time, struggled with all sorts of difficulties and hindrances to gain what we wanted, and at last succeeded in accomplishing our purpose, we feel at first exceedingly glad and satisfied. But as we look closer, and note how our plans work, we generally find that there is a disappointment somewhere, and that things do not turn out exactly as we would have them. Thus it was with Mary Carpenter. It was the experience of years which led her to establish the Kingswood school. She was convinced that what the poor children of the streets needed more than anything was to belong to a family, to feel that they were cared for, and that they must observe rules and regulations as members of happy families always do. When the scheme was floated she was full of hope. She was prepared to put both strength and time into the undertaking. Every moment that could be spared from the ragged school, from her writing, or from home duties, she gave to Kingswood. No weather daunted her. On the coldest, dreariest days she might be seen making her way to the school on foot, for Kingswood was four miles away from Bristol, where she lived, and Mary Carpenter was not wealthy, "it was only by constant personal economy that she could afford to be generous." She arrived there, however, full of energy and enthusiasm, and full of love for the poor little inmates.

With the children her influence was extraordinary. They were never afraid of her ; they always felt that they could appeal to her as to one who was their friend. A little incident reported by herself two or three weeks after the school was opened was quite typical of the children's feeling to her. " When I last went to Kingswood," she said, "a poor little sinner who had been obliged to be locked up, a most dreadful punishment to these wild creatures, when brought out to me, put his little hand on my shoulder, and sobbed out his grievances. The balm of a few kisses quite restored him to a sane state; I felt that the poor little fellow felt that I loved him, and I was thankful for his love."

Can we not from these few words discover something of the secret of Mary Carpenter's influence over the outcasts? "She loved him," he felt that he loved her, and that she was thankful for his love. She even kissed him. Her conduct was very unlike that of some well-meaning but mistaken philanthropists who stand off from the poor, inspect them, lecture them, patronise them, point out their failings and short-comings to them, then look for gratitude and respect from them, but not for love. Mary Carpenter's method was somewhat like that of the best friend the poor ever had, who, when He wanted to help a poor blind man, " *laid His hand on him, and touched him.*"

Yet the inevitable disappointment was waiting for her. It had been a pet idea with Mary Carpenter, with her lofty notions of all the blessing that pertained to family life, that in the substitute for the family which was to be provided in the Reformatory, girls and boys might be brought up together. But after a time she had to confess that this could not be. The girls were more unmanageable than the boys, and when disturbances occurred it was frequently the girls who led the boys into mischief.

In order to understand the difficulties which the managers of Kingswood had to face, it must be remembered that the inmates of reformatories are always law-breakers. Ragged schools are for the destitute and friendless; reformatories are for the criminal. Since, through the efforts of Mary Carpenter, and of people of like mind with her, reformatory schools have been placed under Government, the children who go there are sent by a magistrate, after they have been convicted of some offence against the law, and probably have undergone a short imprisonment. In fact, they are sent to the reformatory where formerly they would have been sent to gaol, but they remain at the reformatory for a term of years, and are not allowed to go away, so that there is hope that they will be rescued from temptation.

But when the Kingswood Reformatory was opened the Reformatory Schools Acts had not been passed; consequently the managers had no legal power to detain the children if they were not willing to stay. All they could do was to influence and persuade them. Some of the children were sent by their parents or by friends, many were sent from a distance, and all were very bad characters. Occasionally, in the early days of the school, it happened that the children resolved to run away, and then parties of them, "led by some more daring spirit, often a girl, would make their way into Bristol to re-visit their old haunts, and to taste the pleasures of city life."

Under these circumstances the distracted master and mistress always came to the managers and Mr. Scott, and to Mary Carpenter, and some of the scenes which were witnessed must have been most extraordinary and disheartening. An idea of them may be gained from an extract from Mary Carpenter's journal. To understand the story it must be understood that Miss Carpenter was most averse to physical force being used. But when the children became absolutely uproarious the police were called in.

" *Saturday, March* 12*th,* 1853. — At 11 a.m. a policeman came to tell me that six girls were then in the station. I told him that it was owing to the excitement caused by the hair-cutting that they had run away. It appeared afterwards that when they were frustrated in their attempt the evening before they darted off the next morning as soon as the gates were open, Martha, Ann, and Marianne, of Cheltenham, being the only ones remaining. Margaret guided them all to her mother's house, who with great presence of mind and discernment of their true interest, locked them together in a room, and sent her younger daughter to the station, whence two policemen were at once sent to fetch them.

"In about an hour I went down with Mr. and Miss A. Instead of finding them in a room waiting for me, as I expected from what the policeman had said, I was told that they were all locked up. The superintendent was most indignant with them ; he

G

said he had never seen such girls. They had insulted the officers, and been so outrageous, that he had given two a slap in the face, and locked them all in separate cells, whence they called out, screamed, and sang in such a manner that those six were enough to corrupt a hundred.

"He then led us to the entrance of the corridor, where I listened to sounds that indeed shocked me, and that revealed the wicked and audacious state in which they were. These cells had doors made of strong iron bars, so that we could see and hear what passed within.

"He then accompanied me to the door of each cell, calling each little girl to the door, as one would call a wild beast to the front of his den. If I had felt any doubt before of the useless and injurious effect of physical coercion, and the force of kindness and moral influence on these poor children, all doubt would have vanished. As I approached each girl, and told her how grieved I was to see her here in such a condition when I had left her good and happy the day before, she hung down her head and was quite softened ; one affectionately took my hand.

"There was now no fear. I requested that they might be released, which was done, and said we would walk with them to the old Market Stand, and thence take flys. The superintendent objected, saying that there were always bad people about who might misunderstand our motives towards the children, and

insult us, or even try to rescue them. I said I was
not afraid of this, for the only time I had been spoken
to was one day when I was taking back three girls,
and as I passed a very low-looking woman said
' God bless ye.' . . .

Here is another extract :—

" *Tuesday, March* 15*th.*—I received, to my dismay,
a note from Mr. Scott, whom I was expecting in
Bristol, stating his desire for my immediate presence,
as he was obliged then to leave Kingswood, and most
of the children were at that moment divided among
the neighbours, confined with their hands tied, in their
respective cellars. I hastened over. Regan (one of
the boys) afterwards told Mr. A. that he was watching in his cellar for the sound of my fly, as he was
sure I should come. Kingswood School was nearly
deserted ; it was long before I could find any official,
as they were all visiting the various culprits.

" It appeared that at prayers that morning Rowan
and another were behaving in a very improper
manner, and were taken out of the room. They were
soon seen through the windows dancing defiantly
about. The infection rapidly spread. The other
children rushed out, and the greater part, both of
boys and girls, ran into the field beyond the bounds,
where they danced about in perfect defiance. Nothing
was to be done but to seize them one by one, tie their
hands, and even their feet, and carry them to the
houses of the neighbours, who all gave their ready

sympathy and help. The morning's work was most painful and harassing.

"I arrived about four, and Mr. Scott departed soon after. It was arranged that while Mr. A. stayed with the remaining boys, and Miss S. with the girls, Mr. Morris should go and bring back the boys by degrees, while I went to the girls. I found them all much softened and subdued, and was very glad to unbind them and bring them home. The evening and the next morning were spent quietly, and all returned to their duty."

On another occasion, when some girls had broken all bounds, and committed an offence for which they had to be taken before the magistrates and sent to prison, Miss Carpenter wrote :—" My poor girls and I wept together while I told them that their own mother did not love them more than I, and that they had now compelled us, in faithfulness to the duty we owed to the Queen, who had committed them to our charge, and to themselves, to give them up to the magistrates to be controlled, as we could not control them ; that I would visit them in prison if allowed, or if not, that my thoughts would be with them ; and that I begged them, as a token of love for me, to go off quietly. They remained quite quiet the whole time till the next day, when they went away as gently with Miss A. to Bristol as if they were going to a pleasure."

It seemed, therefore, that as far as could be seen at present, it would be better that the boys and girls should be separated. It will be remembered that in the lessons which she gave at St. James's Back Miss Carpenter had found that it was pleasanter to teach boys than it was to teach girls. Others had arrived at the same opinion. The boys could be managed—there were gentlemen willing to devote time and attention to them. Little by little they were beginning to get into better order; the encouragements, too, with regard to them were great.

But the condition of the girls was less promising. They made progress, it is true, but "not so much as the boys." Their kind friend mourned over them. On one occasion she said :—" The evil I find out in these poor girls only makes me love them more desperately." At another time :—" I shudder with indignation and intense compassion when I look at our young girls, and behold the fearful condition to which their passions have been brought by ill-treatment."

Still something must be done for them, so it was determined that they should be removed from Kingswood and provided for elsewhere. At one time Miss Carpenter entertained the idea of taking them into her own home, but her friends very naturally were afraid of the additional work and anxiety for her, and did what they could to dissuade her from it. She yielded to their wishes, but she did not give up the resolution to devote herself to the girls.

While Miss Carpenter was considering how the

arrangements which should bring the girls under her personal care should be provided, a fine old Elizabethan house in Bristol, known as the Red Lodge, came into the market. The Red Lodge was in a very bad condition, and the garden was a wilderness, but otherwise it was exactly what was wanted. Miss Carpenter at once appealed to Lady Byron, the kind friend who had helped her before. This generous lady immediately came to her assistance, and bought the house, placing it in Miss Carpenter's hands at a small rent, on condition that she should have it entirely under her own care and be allowed to work it according to her own ideas. Other friends gave the furniture, and in a very short time the institution was fairly started.

Thus was commenced the Red Lodge School, the celebrated home for girls with which the name of Mary Carpenter will for ever be associated. From the very first it was under her sole management; the work done there was carried on under her direction ; the officials were responsible to her, and to the last day of her life she had the entire control of everything connected with it. It was there that her best work was done. By its means hundreds of girls have been rescued from a life of degradation, and trained to live honest sober lives. They and their children are now (in the eloquent words of a writer in the *Times*) " fulfilling the best hopes of the philanthropic woman who, with faith that never wavered, insight that never failed, and love that never wearied, devoted herself for more than twenty years to their welfare."

Sad to say, the new school was scarcely brought into working order when Mary Carpenter was struck down with rheumatic fever, which kept her hanging between life and death, and seriously affected her heart. The Red Lodge was opened before Christmas; it was April before its mistress was able to take pen in hand; May before she was able even to visit the schools; and the summer was far advanced before work could be resumed. The school itself did not actually suffer, for Mary's sister Anna looked after its management, and filled as well as she could her sister's place. But it was a great trial of patience, and unfortunately, as far as health was concerned, it left effects which remained through life.

When at length restored health enabled her to resume her post as manager of the Red Lodge, Miss Carpenter took up her work with the greatest enthusiasm. She was by nature specially fitted to act as a juvenile reformer. She believed in children, she had intense sympathy with them; it was part of her faith that "there is a holy spot in every child's heart," and this holy spot she was very quick to find out.

The work at Red Lodge was full of interest, but it required a great deal of patience; indeed no one who has not actually laboured amongst the depraved and criminal can imagine how discouragements and disappointments were every-day affairs. But Mary

Carpenter's love for the children never wearied. Mrs. Nassau Senior once said, "What these girls needed was 'mothering;'" and it was 'mothering' which Mary Carpenter tried to give them. On certain nights she used to go round to them after they were in bed, talk to them quietly, and kiss them before she left them— a beautiful motherly act. Yet she never allowed her sympathy to run to waste, and to degenerate into weak sentiment. She was quite aware of the children's faults, and she was never taken in by protestations of affection or sham promises of amendment. When they fell back into sin she mourned over them with intensest grief.

Mrs. Hind, of Dartmouth Park Hill, a lady who worked under Miss Carpenter for some time, has kindly furnished a little descriptive sketch of this noble lady at this time which is full of interest.

Mrs. Hind says: "I worked under Miss Carpenter in Bristol from 1852 to 1856, being one of a band of young people who were attracted by her influence and fired by her example. We loved as well as respected her, and in my own case the feeling entertained was one almost of reverence; for from childhood the name of Carpenter was to me one of good repute indeed, in the highest sense.

"I think, however, we all stood in a little awe of her; but so did not the street arabs for whom she worked. Of them, indeed, one might say they loved her because she first loved them; and I have seen them on holiday occasions gather round her as children gather round a loving mother. Their queer quaint ways and sayings amused her, as much as their wretched condition grieved her. For in her was a fund of humorous perception which might not have been guessed by those who saw her in her graver aspects, and I think it helped her sometimes on her toilsome way. She was so large-minded, too, as to enjoy even innocent raillery directed against herself; and to give up small details of management, as when she deferred to my mother in the domestic arrangement at Red Lodge. There was nothing little about her, but much that was childlike, as with all great natures. And her varied culture and early experience in the tuition of young ladies kept her mind open to general interests, and prevented her devotion to the ' good cause,' as she called it, becoming narrowed and bigoted.

"Miss Carpenter was certainly exacting, and was perhaps too ready to assume in others the strong will and power of endurance which characterised herself. But the only thing which moved her to anger was *unreliability*, the ready promise without the performance. To those who really tried, however imperfectly, to help her, she was most lenient and most grateful.

"The quality which most impressed every one in her countenance, voice, and manner, and in everything she did, was intense earnestness. It was literally true of her, that whatever she found to do she did it with her might. She threw into the Sunday school, the Dorcas Society, or what not, the same concentration of purpose and undivided attention that were required for much larger and more public matters ; and the entire absence of self-consciousness was the same wherever she was and in whatever company.

"Her other most marked characteristic was, I think, religiousness—pure and simple. Free from any suspicion of cant, it was yet plainly to be seen that, like Enoch, she walked with God, and from Him derived her strength and unfailing hope.

"Her family affections were very strong, and I well remember how when a near and dear relative who had hitherto worked with her was about to marry, she said in her quaint way, half reproachfully, half humorously, 'It is really wonderful how readily dear —— has taken up the idea of matrimony.' For she knew that the said 'idea,' when carried out, would in most cases prove a loss to the 'good cause.'

"But there was nothing sour, nothing 'old maidish' about her. Indeed, she was a very woman, large-hearted and high-souled, and one whose like those who remember her can hardly expect to look upon again."

About two years after the opening of the Red Lodge, Mrs. Carpenter, Mary's mother, with whom she lived, died. This was a great trial. Mrs. Carpenter was a broad-spirited, noble woman. She had sympathised with and helped her husband in his public work, and when he was taken away she had sympathised with and encouraged her daughter. During the last months of her life, when health had begun to fail, and she was obliged to be considered an invalid, she had always been ready to listen with eager interest to the story of the day's work, pleased if things had gone well, and sad if there had been disappointment. Earnest workers, and especially philanthropic workers, are generally very dependent on sympathy of this sort. It is very hard to keep on day after day *alone.* The thought that there is some one who will rejoice when we rejoice, and sorrow when we sorrow, is encouraging, and sometimes it seems as if those who do nothing but approve and sympathise help almost as much as those who toil and strive. Yet none but those who have once had this perfect sympathy can understand what it must be to lose it.

The loss was specially felt by Mary Carpenter, because she was the sort of person who was so occupied with the large needs of the community that she forgot her own small needs ; so that without her mother she felt almost lost. In writing to her brother a few weeks after her mother's death, she said, " Now that I contrast more the daily life with what it used to be with my beloved mother in the drawing-room, always ready to welcome and to sympathise, to be cared for and to care, and feeling that I could conduce to her happiness, and was sure of her loving kiss and blessing, I have of course felt more painfully the desolation and irreparable loss." At another time she said, "People don't like me to tire myself, but it is better to come home ready to drop, and to go to bed and to sleep at once, than to have time to feel the dreadful loneliness of this large house, once so peopled, and all the loved ones gone. All my old haunts and places are altered and gone ; I seem plunged alone into a new life."

Some idea of the extent to which Mary's mother had been accustomed to look after her may be gained from a story which is told of how, one bitterly cold day, Mr. Matthew Davenport Hill met Mrs. Carpenter in the street. He told her that she ought not to be out in such weather, on which she said, "She was obliged to come out to buy clothes for Mary, for she never would buy anything for herself, and had really nothing to put on." Miss Cobbe, too, has told us that Miss Carpenter was simply indifferent to all the minor comforts of life, so much so that she could not comprehend any one caring much for them. Once when she had been staying two or three days at a country house, she gravely remarked, " The ladies and gentlemen all came down dressed for dinner, and evidently thought the meal rather a pleasant part of the day." Unlike these eccentric ladies and gentlemen her own custom was to take whatever could be most easily prepared, and she scarcely gave herself time to eat her food. In the days when she used to go to the Red Lodge she always breakfasted during the winter months before daylight, and rushed off to work as soon as ever the meal was over. Every minute of the day had its allotted task, and rest and food were quite subordinate affairs.

Later Miss Carpenter must have discovered the mistake of this kind of self-neglect, for she altered her habits, and though still exceedingly simple in her tastes, was most particular to take her meals at regular and stated intervals. A lady who knew her well three or four years before her death, in writing about her said, "When with us she would see friends all the morning, address a meeting in the afternoon, and go out to dinner in the evening; but twice between times must come the fifteen minutes' rest and the beef tea. One evening, when two or three gentlemen had each an appointment with her, she said to the first, after the business part of his visit was ended, 'I think that is all you need of me, sir!' and bowing to the puzzled man, went to obtain a few minutes' rest before the arrival of her next visitor. Afterwards speaking of it apologetically, she said, 'I must do so, or I should accomplish nothing.' Another proof of her changed habit is found in a letter to a friend who had just attained her threescore and ten years. Miss Carpenter says, 'You have, I hope, found out the secret of preserving health, which keeps me well, viz., to ascertain the measure of your strength and not to attempt to go beyond it, but to accept all the little indulgences which we did not allow ourselves in younger life, but which are now lawfully our due.' "

In this case as in most others, the lesson taught by experience was of highest value, and girls who want to do good work in the world would be wise to remember it. Those workers do the best service who work reasonably; who remember that energy and steadfastness are largely dependent upon health, and that health is largely dependent upon obedience to laws which can never be disregarded with impunity. Enthusiasm which leads its possessor to forget common sense is a weakness.

After her mother's death Mary Carpenter was left really without any home ties; she was therefore entirely at liberty to devote herself to her work. This was all the easier because she had a little money, as much as sufficed for her moderate wants. For a short time she took up her abode with her married sister; but though her friends did their utmost to make her happy, she was not content with this. She longed above everything to have a small home of her own, where she could have workers for the poor living with her, employing girls who needed special care to do the housework. The plan was an excellent one, but it did not at first seem practicable.

Towards the close of the year 1857, however, a suitable house, overlooking Red Lodge, and separated from it only by a narrow street, became vacant. Lady

Byron purchased it, and in a short time Miss Carpenter removed into it. Some time before this a small cottage near Red Lodge had been secured, and this was fitted up as a laundry. The methods adopted were very simple. Red Lodge was occupied by girls of the criminal class, young thieves and desperate characters who had been rescued from their state of degradation. Necessarily the discipline which had to be maintained over these girls was strict ; yet there was always held out to them the hope that if they behaved well and proved themselves worthy of trust, they should in time be promoted to "the College," where they would be called upon to do responsible work, and trained as domestic servants. The girls in the Lodge had a great respect for the girls in the College; they looked up to them as respectable individuals, and tried to behave decently and quietly in order that they might win the reward of being placed among them. If the girls at the College misbehaved they were sent back to the Lodge, and this was felt to be a great disgrace.

After removing to her new home Miss Carpenter established a still higher order of merit. The girls at the College were told that if they proved themselves worthy of the honour, they might in time be chosen to live in Miss Carpenter's own house, and act as her little maids. They would then be treated exactly like ordinary domestics, sent to the town on errands, trusted with money, and allowed as much liberty as other young servants. If they answered to this trust it was understood that when the period for which they were sentenced had expired, Miss Carpenter would recommend them to good situations, and so after all their failure and mistake they would win for themselves an honoured position once more. Miss Carpenter was known to be very watchful and strict as a mistress; she was kindness itself, but she was not weak. She never gave a recommendation unless it was deserved, she was exceedingly quick to notice any irregularity; therefore a character from her was worth having.

This simple system of rewards and punishments was a great success, and by its means hundreds of girls, unhappily degraded and apparently lost to all sense of self-respect, were won to the paths of honesty and virtue. Their salvation was the work of Miss Carpenter's life, it was to their welfare she devoted herself, it was for them she worked and prayed. For more than twenty years this heroic woman toiled and prayed in order that she might pluck these poor castaways as brands from the burning. It was for this that her name is now reverenced as one of the noblest of the World's Workers.

Yet it must not be thought that the work at Red Lodge, interesting though it was, occupied all her time. On the contrary; she was most energetic and unwearied in taking steps to get good laws passed which should benefit these helpless little ones. A great

part of her life was spent in trying to convince people
of the wisdom of her plans, and to persuade them to
give them a trial. She attended conferences, wrote
books and pamphlets, corresponded first with one
statesman and then another, but never rested until
she had carried her point. There was no silencing
her when once she saw clearly that a certain step
ought to be taken. She left no stone unturned till
her end was accomplished. She has quite reasonably
been likened to the widow in the parable of the Un-
just Judge—she compelled the law-makers to listen
to her. Through her importunity and her earnestness
she had power with them and prevailed.

Descriptions of Acts of Parliament are not very
interesting reading, excepting for people trained to
understand such things, therefore of this part of her
work it will not be well to enter into detail here. It will
be sufficient to say that it was largely owing to Mary
Carpenter and her supporters that valuable and important measures, such as the Reformatory Schools
Act, were passed, according to which children convicted
of crime were sent to reformatories instead of to gaol.
The Industrial Schools Bill, which enabled magistrates
to place in Industrial Schools neglected boys found
in the streets, had a similar origin. Her interest and
energy in altering and improving the laws which
affected the condition of children extended over a
period of thirty years. During this time she wrote a
very large number of letters to statesmen and various

H

influential personages, giving suggestions and supplying information on various points. All this required much patience, and very often was very wearying work. To use her own words, " she had to write the same thing backwards and forwards, and crossways, and every way possible, to try to get things, or rather one simple thing, into people's heads." But "happily she had the patience of Job."

Her zeal on behalf of neglected children was indeed absolutely without bounds, and could not abate until something was done for them. As her friend Mr. Commissioner Hill said of her, "she was like a boy running down Greenwich Hill—she had lost the power of slackening her pace, and must go to the bottom."

Working constantly in the reformatory, and coming constantly as she did into communication with young thieves and vagabonds, Mary Carpenter soon saw that child-criminals were not the only children who needed to be helped, but that there were children belonging to a class just above the criminals who were as yet comparatively innocent, but who would almost certainly become criminal if they were not looked after and cared for. It was to reach these neglected little ones that the " Industrial Schools Act" was planned and carried out, an Act which made it lawful for a magistrate to send ragged children who lived in the streets—"street arabs" as they were called, because they were so wild and careless—

to school for a long term. If these children had been sent to reformatories they would have had to mix with companions more degraded than themselves ; if they had been sent to ordinary national or British schools they would have done harm to the manageable, respectable children attending there. What was wanted was that they should be sent to industrial schools, where they could be brought into habits of order, and taught a trade, and given a chance to become respectable members of society.

The Industrial Schools Act was passed in 1857, and immediately Miss Carpenter established a school of the sort required in Bristol. Here boys who would, if left alone, have undoubtedly fallen into trouble and disgrace, were trained and cared for, and as they became old enough to work for their own living were placed in situations and given a fair start in life. Many of these boys were sent abroad and settled in Canada and the United States. There never seemed to be any difficulty in providing for them after they had passed through this school, because gentlemen in business had such confidence in Miss Carpenter's system of education. Numbers of boys were in this way saved from destruction, and turned into respectable members of society.

For years Mary Carpenter was exceedingly busy as a writer. She was the author not only of books, but of innumerable pamphlets and treatises on the subject which engrossed her life. Her first important work was on reformatory schools ; her second was on "Juvenile Delinquents ; " another one, published in 1864, was entitled "Our Convicts." This work was highly valued by people who understood the subject, and it was "honoured "—to use Miss Carpenter's own words—in being placed by the Pope on the Index Expurgatorius, which is a list of books not allowed to be read by Roman Catholics until certain passages have been taken out.

Yet it must not be supposed that in trying to supply the needs of the children this wonderful woman entirely forgot the parents. Her book on "Our Convicts " was really an attempt to apply to grown-up criminals the treatment which she had found answered so well for children. She was particularly concerned for female convicts, and did all that in her lay by establishing refuges, and in other ways, to bring about the regeneration of the misguided and neglected.

It will be remembered that when in early life Mary Carpenter had made the resolve that she would give her life to the work of aiding the miserable and destitute, that she had been much under the influence of two good men—one, Dr. Tuckerman, of America, the other, Rammohun Roy, of India. Dr. Tuckerman had made her feel how much neglected and destitute children needed assistance ; Rammohun Roy had spoken of the hardships endured by women of his country. To the work pointed out by Dr.

Tuckerman Mary Carpenter gave earnest thought and labour during the best years of her life. The interest in the native races of India which had been roused by Rammohun Roy had during this time been necessarily put on one side ; there was no opportunity of taking any step in this direction.

But Mary Carpenter was a woman who could not disregard a claim which had once been "brought home " to her, and those who knew her well were not astonished when, late in life, having done what she could to assist the neglected and destitute children of England, she once more turned her thoughts to the condition of the women of India. At this time Miss Carpenter was nearly sixty years of age, her hair was white, her health was not good (for she never entirely recovered from the effects of the serious illness she passed through soon after the Red Lodge Reformatory was opened, yet her energy and determination were as strong as ever. She made up her mind to go to India, acquaint herself with the facts concerning education, the position of women, the discipline of prisons, and similar subjects, and see whether something could not be done to bring about desirable improvements.

Most people who had accomplished what Mary Carpenter had done, and arrived at her age, would have felt that they had earned a little rest, and allowed a gigantic task like this to be taken up by some one younger and less weary than themselves.

But Mary Carpenter was not at all like "most people." The work was there, and needed to be done. Her own particular work, the management of Red Lodge, of the Industrial and Ragged Schools, could be carried on for a while without her, and so she never thought of holding back. There were great difficulties in the way of her carrying out her intention, but as she once playfully said of herself, she was like Napoleon, for " her the impossible did not exist." She did not feel old ; once when she saw herself described in the papers as "this venerable lady," she was quite shocked, and she felt a strong conviction that she could be of use. She thought a "call" had been given to her, and she resolved to follow it.

Her resolution was strengthened by the visits of several highly educated Hindoos who came over to England and visited Bristol in order to inspect her institutions. From them she learnt how much there was to be done ; their conversation reminded her of Rammohun Roy, and she longed to be in a position to carry out his wishes. When they were told what she was thinking of doing they naturally did all they could to encourage her. A lady who knew Calcutta well said to her, " Oh, that you could go to India, Miss Carpenter ! you are just the person to help the ladies." This was a very general feeling amongst people who knew India ; whilst Miss Carpenter came to feel that if she could carry back to the country of

Rammohun Roy some of the inspiration she had received from him she would be content.

One more institution, however, was to owe its origin to her before she went away. The Certified Industrial School which had been established had been intended for boys only. Miss Carpenter never forgot the girls; so before she quitted Bristol for India she invited a number of ladies to her house and laid before them a plan for a Girls' Industrial School. " I said to them," she afterwards related— " I said to them, ' This must be done, and you are to do it.' " And they did it. A committee was formed ; a house was taken ; the school was opened, and was successfully carried on.

Miss Carpenter visited India four times. Her stay on each occasion did not exceed a few months, but she was very busy during the time. She had a very clear idea of what she wanted to do ; she wanted to inquire into the condition of female education, and see whether something could not be done to raise it ; to look into and report upon the management of reformatory schools, and to investigate the state of the prisons. In short, the subjects which had interested her in England were the subjects which attracted her in India.

Her experiment was made under very favourable circumstances. The Home Government helped her, and made arrangements for her to inspect various public institutions, and to obtain information from official persons. The natives of India, too, were very grateful to her for that kindness and sympathy she was showing them. Some of the ladies were most enthusiastic about her. They thought it wonderful she should take such a journey on their account. One lady in particular expressed the opinion that Miss Carpenter "ought to be adored." The official English, however, were rather shocked, and thought her bold and revolutionary. Scarcely any of the English ladies would come near her, and seemed quite afraid of her. One day news was brought to her that "a whole sermon was preached against her in one of the churches." Adverse criticism of this kind never made Miss Carpenter stop in her career for a single instant. She said, " That sort of thing does not matter. I am used to it."

So far as education was concerned her great desire was to establish female normal schools, where women could be trained to act as teachers to their own sex. She established some of these schools, and on the occasion of her second visit to India she even took the post of lady superintendent, and engaged in the work of instruction. It was indeed wonderful that so many years ago she perceived the existence of evils which the reformers of to-day are only now beginning to remedy, namely, the evils which arise from the early marriage of Hindoo women, their enforced widowhood, and the sufferings they endure from the want of medical assistance. Years after Miss

Carpenter signed a memorial to the senate of the University of London, praying them to bestow medical degrees upon women ; and she then stated that during her four visits to India she had learnt that it was a great misfortune for Hindoo women that there were no female doctors.

Yet it can scarcely be said that either with regard to female education, or the management of reformatories and prisons, Miss Carpenter achieved a great success in India. Her reforms were too advanced for the times. They were on the right lines, and it is to be hoped that in the future they will be carried out. They were appreciated also by the natives of the highest rank and education, many of whom hardly knew how to express their enthusiasm and respect for the noble lady who had suggested them. It is true they were partly successful. The good seed was sown, and some of these days it will bring forth an abundant harvest. Lord Dufferin was right when he said, after hearing an account of Miss Carpenter's work in India, " India is a great country, and the history of a great country deals only with important events; but I am certain that when the history of that country during the present century is being written the visit of Miss Carpenter to its shores will not be left unrecorded."

Miss Carpenter was herself very hopeful about the results of her work in India. On the occasion of her last visit to that country, which took place ten years after her first visit, and when she was nearly seventy years old, she noticed that very great progress had been made amongst women during the course of ten years. She saw that education was spreading amongst women of the lower class. She believed that she had accomplished what she had sought to do in going out, and witnessed what she regarded as the complete success of her principles and system. Writing to a friend, she said, "The work *will* go on. In faith and hope I can say ' India, farewell.'" Writing to another friend about her work in India, she said, " My mind will be satisfied if it can be said of me in this as in other matters, ' She hath done what she could.'"

This wish to earn the right to have it said of her, " She hath done what she could," was expressed more than once by Mary Carpenter. Indeed, if the words could not be applied with truth to her, there are few women of whom they could be spoken. Truly, she accomplished marvels. During the intervals of her visits to India she was busy looking after the working of the different institutions which she had originated. These formed a remarkable group. There was the Ragged School, which had been begun in St. James's Back, and which had now been turned into a day industrial feeding school. Associated with this was the "Children's Agency," established for the purpose of keeping a kindly oversight over the discharged inmates of other schools, and helping them to find work and situations ; also to seek out young vagrants who might be brought under training. There was a Workmen's Hall, containing a lecture hall and library, intended to provide a place of simple entertainment and recreation ; near this was a Boys' Home with lodging for between twenty and thirty boys. There was the Reformatory School at Kingswood, and the Girls' Reformatory in the Red Lodge, with the cottage adjoining, to which girls were promoted who showed that they were deserving of trust. There was the Certified Industrial School for Boys, which had been established and conducted for two years by Miss Carpenter herself, and the Girls' Certified Industrial School, established by a band of ladies at Miss Carpenter's suggestion just before she sailed for India. Each of these had been most useful, and all, with the exception of the Workmen's Hall, had been planned to rescue destitute and neglected children, who but for her would have been left to perish.

In early life, her biographer tells us, Miss Carpenter had longed for the happiness of being a wife and a mother. Later she became content that her affection could be freely given to those who needed it. " There is a verse in the prophecies," she once wrote, " ' I have given thee children whom thou hast not borne,' and the motherly love of my heart has been given to many who have never known before a mother's love, and I have thanked God for it." In another letter she said :—" It is quite striking to observe how much the useful power and influence of woman has developed of late years. Unattached ladies, such as widows and unmarried women, have quite ample work to do in the world for the good of others to absorb all their powers. Wives and mothers have a very noble work given them by God, and want no more."

Mary Carpenter, like Mary Somerville, was strongly in favour of women having the franchise. When first she began her work she did not care very much for this—she was so very womanly that she was afraid of feminine modesty being destroyed by women taking part in public affairs. Sometimes, when she was spoken to on the subject, she playfully evaded the difficulty by saying, " I don't talk about my rights, I take them," or she would declare that she had all the rights she wanted given to her. But as she grew older her opinions on this question changed. She signed a petition for the enfranchisement of women ; in her last years she frequently expressed her belief that women ought to be allowed to vote on the same terms as men ; and Miss Cobbe tells us that on one occasion she took her place on the platform, and either proposed or seconded one of the resolutions demanding the franchise, adding a few words of cordial approval.

Another of her characteristics ought not to be forgotten. She was exceedingly devoted to the Royal Family, and had a most enthusiastic admiration for the Queen. She said the Queen was a " noble and lovely woman," and that "she always had felt a warm sympathy with her beautiful domestic character." When the Prince of Wales was married she was quite joyful, and followed all the details of preparation with most devoted interest, and she said to a friend, " What a love that family has given to our country! what a heart!" Once she had the honour of an interview with the Queen, and was presented by her Majesty with her " Leaves from our Journal in the Highlands," on the fly-leaf of which . was written, "Mary Carpenter, from Victoria R." Miss Carpenter was delighted with this, and also much encouraged by the Queen taking an interest in her work. In relating the story of her visit to Windsor afterwards, she said :—" People have asked me if I did not feel nervous. I was not in the least so. I was not going for myself, but for the women of India." During this interview the Queen took a Scotch pebble bracelet from her own arm and clasped it on that of Mary Carpenter. This bracelet she valued most highly.

It would have been a sad thing if the old age of a woman like Mary Carpenter had not been happy and peaceful. But it was eminently so. For a little while after her return from her third journey to India she felt very lonely. Her sister Anna, who had been her companion and support through all her work, was dead ; her friends were afraid to visit her, because they had learnt to think she was always busy, and would not care to be interrupted, so that sometimes she passed whole days in solitude. Many a night at this time she passed in sleeplessness, and sometimes she had to stop work because she was weeping. The remedy she sought for this state of things was very characteristic of her. She determined to adopt some children. She remembered two little Hindoo boys whose parents would, she believed, be glad to have her take charge of them, and when returning from her fourth visit to India she brought these boys back with her. After this she was quite happy again. The fact was that she was possessed of the mother heart, she felt a want unless there was a child near her whom she could cherish. With children by her side the desolation of loneliness never came over her.

The last days of her life were very bright and peaceful. She still continued to work, and her mind was as clear and active as ever. A letter which she wrote to a friend who had completed her eightieth birthday is so beautiful that it deserves to be copied :—

"MY DEAR FRIEND,—I was very happy to see you so bright and serene at the age which in the olden time, before our blessed Lord came, was 'labour and sorrow.' I, too, am able to rejoice evermore.

"I am truly thankful that, though I cannot do much walking, I can get through really as much as ever in *intensity* if not in *quantity*, often in the latter. I am also very happy to have enough money to do all I want. Few people can say that. I am not obliged to stint myself, and I can indulge myself in making my places and things very nice, and binding books and making presents, and subscribing to good objects and taking journeys. I am only stingy in things which I do not like spending money about. So I am rich. And I have, after thirty years, got the Government to attend to the miserable children! And so we both thank God."

In another letter written to her nephew, she said—

"I do not look back with sorrow on the past. There have been many painful woundings, and sad bereavements, and great struggles, and dark perplexities, but they have all blended together to make a calm whole of the past, very wonderfully calm when I think of parts alone. As you say, there has been one deep moving spirit running through all. I used often to desire to have

' A soul by force of sorrows high,
Uplifted to the purest sky
Of undisturbed humanity.'

" Now I do not seek that or anything, but thankfully take whatever is given. 'She hath done what she could,' I can truly say of myself, whatever errors I have fallen into. So I look very serenely back from this boundary, and hopefully to what remains of life, the brightest and best of all, and most full of blessings."

A little more than a month after writing this letter

she received the news of the death of her youngest brother. It was a great shock. About a month later, on Thursday, June 14th, 1877, she wrote proposing to visit her brother, Dr. W. B. Carpenter, in London. She was busy all day after doing this, and in the evening she happened to meet in the street one of her Parliamentary friends. With him she conversed for a little while on public topics with great earnestness of feeling and clearness of thought. She then went into her quiet study and wrote till a later hour than usual. When she was last seen it was with a smile upon her face. She lay down to rest and slept, and before the dawn she had passed quietly away.

Mary Carpenter, when a little child, scarcely able to talk, amused her friends by saying she " wanted to be ooseful." She died at the age of seventy, having accomplished as noble a work as ever was given to woman.

(Our Portrait of Miss Carpenter is copied, by permission, from a Photograph by C. Voss Bark, Clifton.)

PRINTED BY CASSELL & COMPANY, LIMITED, LA BELLE SAUVAGE, LONDON, E.C.

Illustrated, Fine-Art, and other Volumes.

Abbeys and Churches of England and Wales, The: Descriptive, Historical, Pictorial. 21s.

Adventure, The World of. Fully Illustrated. Yearly Vol. 9s.

American Library of Fiction. Crown 8vo, cloth, 3s. 6d. each.

A Latin-Quarter Courtship. By Henry Harland (Sidney Luska).

Grandison Mather. By Henry Harland (Sidney Luska).

"Æp." By Edgar Henry.

The Tragedy of Brinkwater. By Martha L. Moodey.

Karmel the Scout. By Sylvanus Cobb, Junr.

Orion the Gold Beater. By Sylvanus Cobb, Junr.

American Yachts and Yachting. Illustrated. 6s.

Arabian Nights Entertainments, Cassell's Pictorial. 10s. 6d.

Architectural Drawing. By Phené Spiers. Illustrated. 10s. 6d.

Art, The Magazine of. Yearly Vol. With 12 Photogravures, Etchings, &c., and several hundred choice Engravings. 16s.

Bashkirtseff, Marie, The Journal of. Two Vols., demy 8vo, 24s.

Birds' Nests, Eggs, and Egg-Collecting. By R. Kearton. Illustrated with 16 Coloured Plates. 5s.

Bismarck, Prince. By Charles Lowe, M.A. Two Vols. 10s. 6d.

Black Arrow, The. A Tale of the Two Roses. By R. L. Stevenson. 5s.

British Ballads. With 275 Original Illustrations. Two Vols. 7s. 6d. each.

British Battles on Land and Sea. By James Grant. With about 600 Illustrations. Three Vols., 4to, £1 7s.; Library Edition, £1 10s.

British Battles, Recent. Illustrated. 4to, 9s.; Library Edition, 10s.

British Empire, The. By Sir George Campbell, M.P. 3s.

Browning, An Introduction to the Study of. By A. Symons. 2s. 6d.

Butterflies and Moths, European. With 61 Coloured Plates. 35s.

Canaries and Cage-Birds, The Illustrated Book of. With 56 Facsimile Coloured Plates, 35s. Half-morocco, £2 5s.

Cannibals and Convicts. By Julian Thomas ("The Vagabond"). 5s.

Captain Trafalgar. By Westall and Laurie. 5s.

Cassell's Family Magazine. Yearly Vol. Illustrated. 9s.

Celebrities of the Century. 21s.; Roxburgh, 25s.

Choice Dishes at Small Cost. By A. G. Payne. 1s.

Cities of the World. Four Vols. Illustrated. 7s. 6d. each.

Civil Service, Guide to Employment in the. 3s. 6d.

Civil Service.—Guide to Female Employment in Government Offices. 1s.

Clinical Manuals for Practitioners and Students of Medicine. A List of Volumes forwarded post free on application to the Publishers.

Clothing, The Influence of, on Health. By F. Treves, F.R.C.S. 2s.

Colour. By Prof. A. H. Church. With Coloured Plates. 3s. 6d.

Columbus, Christopher. By Washington Irving. Three Vols. 7s. 6d.

Commerce, The Year-Book of. 5s.

Commodore Junk. By G. Manville Fenn. 5s.

Conquests of the Cross. With numerous Illustrations. Vol. I., 9s.

Cookery, A Year's. By Phyllis Browne. 3s. 6d.

Cookery, Cassell's Dictionary of. Containing about Nine Thousand Recipes. 7s. 6d.; Roxburgh, 10s. 6d.

Cookery, Cassell's Popular. With Four Coloured Plates. Cloth gilt, 2s.

Cookery, Cassell's Shilling. 384 pages, limp cloth, 1s.

Countries of the World, The. By Robert Brown, M.A., Ph.D., &c. Complete in Six Vols., with about 750 Illustrations. 4to, 7s. 6d. each.

Cromwell, Oliver. By J. ALLANSON PICTON, M.P. 5s.

Culmshire Folk. By the Author of "John Orlebar," &c. 3s. 6d.

Cyclopædia, Cassell's Concise. With 12,000 subjects, brought down to the latest date. With about 600 Illustrations, 15s.; Roxburgh, 18s.

Cyclopædia, Cassell's Miniature. Containing 30,000 subjects. 3s. 6d.

Dairy Farming. By Prof. J. P. SHELDON. With 25 Coloured Plates. 21s.

Dead Man's Rock. A Romance. By Q. 5s.

Dickens, Character Sketches from. FIRST, SECOND, and THIRD SERIES. With Six Original Drawings in each by F. BARNARD. In Portfolio, 21s. each.

Dog, Illustrated Book of the. By VERO SHAW, B.A. With 28 Coloured Plates. Cloth levelled, 35s.; half-morocco, 45s.

Dog Stories and Dog Lore. By Col. THOS. W. KNOX. 6s.

Dog, The. By IDSTONE. Illustrated. 2s. 6d.

Domestic Dictionary, The. Illustrated. Cloth, 7s. 6d.

Doré Gallery, The. With 250 Illustrations by DORÉ. 4to, 42s.

Doré's Dante's Inferno. Illustrated by GUSTAVE DORÉ. 21s.

Doré's Dante's Purgatorio and Paradiso. Illustrated by DORÉ. 21s.

Doré's Milton's Paradise Lost. Illustrated by DORÉ. 4to, 21s.

Earth, Our, and its Story. By Dr. ROBERT BROWN, F.L.S. With Coloured Plates and numerous Wood Engravings. Three Vols. 9s. each.

Edinburgh, Old and New. With 600 Illustrations. Three Vols. 9s. each.

Egypt: Descriptive, Historical, and Picturesque. By Prof. G. EBERS. With 800 Original Engravings. *Popular Edition.* In Two Vols. 42s.

"89." A Novel. By EDGAR HENRY. Cloth, 3s. 6d.

Electricity, Age of. By PARK BENJAMIN, Ph.D. 7s. 6d.

Electricity, Practical. By Prof. W. E. AYRTON. 7s. 6d.

Encyclopædic Dictionary, The. A New and Original Work of Reference to all the Words in the English Language. Complete in Fourteen Divisional Vols., 10s. 6d. each; or Seven Vols., half-morocco, 21s. each; half-russia, 25s.

England, Cassell's Illustrated History of. With 2,000 Illustrations. Ten Vols., 4to, 9s. each. *Revised Edition.* Vols. I., II., and III., 9s. each.

English History, The Dictionary of. *Cheap Edition.* 10s. 6d.

English Literature, Dictionary of. By W. DAVENPORT ADAMS. *Cheap Edition*, 7s. 6d.; Roxburgh, 10s. 6d.

English Literature, Library of. By Prof. HENRY MORLEY.

> VOL. I.—SHORTER ENGLISH POEMS. 7s. 6d.
> VOL. II.—ILLUSTRATIONS OF ENGLISH RELIGION. 7s. 6d.
> VOL III.—ENGLISH PLAYS. 7s. 6d.
> VOL IV.—SHORTER WORKS IN ENGLISH PROSE. 7s. 6d.
> VOL. V.—SKETCHES OF LONGER WORKS IN ENGLISH VERSE AND PROSE. 7s. 6d.

English Literature, Morley's First Sketch of. *Revised Edition*, 7s. 6d.

English Literature, The Story of. By ANNA BUCKLAND. 3s. 6d.

English Writers. By Prof. HENRY MORLEY. Vols. I. to V. 5s. each.

Æsop's Fables. Illustrated throughout by ERNEST GRISET. Cloth. 3s. 6d.

Etching. By S. K. KOEHLER. With 30 Full-Page Plates. £4 4s.

Etiquette of Good Society. 1s.; cloth, 1s. 6d.

Europe, Pocket Guide to, Cassell's. Leather. 6s.

Eye, Ear, and Throat, The Management of the. 3s. 6d.

Family Physician, The. By Eminent PHYSICIANS and SURGEONS, *New and Revised Edition.* Cloth, 21s.; Roxburgh, 25s.

Fenn, G. Manville, Works by. Boards, 2s. each; cloth, 2s. 6d. each.

MY PATIENTS. Being the Notes of a Navy Surgeon.	THE PARSON o' DUMFORD.
DUTCH THE DIVER.	THE VICAR'S PEOPLE. } In cloth only.
	SWEET MACE.

POVERTY CORNER.

Field Naturalist's Handbook, The. By the Rev. J. G. WOOD and Rev. THEODORE WOOD. 5s.

Figuier's Popular Scientific Works. With Several Hundred Illustrations in each. 3s. 6d. each.

THE HUMAN RACE.	THE OCEAN WORLD.
REPTILES AND BIRDS.	THE INSECT WORLD.

MAMMALIA.

Fine-Art Library, The. Edited by JOHN SPARKES, Principal of the South Kensington Art Schools. Each Book contains about 100 Illustrations. 5s. each.

ENGRAVING.	THE EDUCATION OF THE ARTIST.
TAPESTRY.	(Non-illustrated.)
THE ENGLISH SCHOOL OF PAINT-ING.	GREEK ARCHÆOLOGY.
THE FLEMISH SCHOOL OF PAINT-ING.	ARTISTIC ANATOMY.
	THE DUTCH SCHOOL OF PAINTING.

Flora's Feast: a Masque of Flowers. With Coloured Designs by WALTER CRANE. 5s.

Flower Painting in Water Colours. With Coloured Plates. First and Second Series. 5s. each.

Flower Painting, Elementary. With Eight Coloured Plates. 3s.

Flowers, and How to Paint Them. By MAUD NAFTEL. With Coloured Plates. 5s.

Forging of the Anchor, The. A Poem. By Sir SAMUEL FERGUSON, LL.D. With 20 Original Illustrations. Gilt edges, 5s.

Fossil Reptiles, A History of British. By Sir RICHARD OWEN, K.C.B., F.R.S., &c. With 268 Plates. In Four Vols., £12 12s.

France as It Is. By ANDRÉ LEBON and PAUL PELET. With Three Maps. Crown 8vo, cloth, 7s. 6d.

Fresh-water Fishes of Europe, The. By Prof. H. G. SEELEY, F.R.S. *Cheap Edition.* 7s. 6d.

Garden Flowers, Familiar. By SHIRLEY HIBBERD. With Coloured Plates by F. E. HULME, F.L.S. Complete in Five Series. 12s. 6d. each.

Gardening, Cassell's Popular. Illustrated. 4 vols., 5s. each.

Gas, The Art of Cooking by. By Mrs. SUGG. Illustrated. Cloth, 2s. 6d.

Gaudeamus. One Hundred Songs for Schools and Colleges. Edited by JOHN FARMER. 5s.

Geometrical Drawing for Army Candidates. By H. T. LILLEY, M.A. 2s.

Geometry, First Elements of Experimental. By PAUL BERT. 1s. 6d.

Geometry, Practical Solid. By MAJOR ROSS. 2s.

Germany, William of. By ARCHIBALD FORBES. Cloth, 3s. 6d.

Gleanings from Popular Authors. Two Vols. With Original Illustrations. 4to, 9s. each. Two Vols. in One, 15s.

Great Painters of Christendom, The, from Cimabue to Wilkie. By JOHN FORBES-ROBERTSON. Illustrated throughout. 10s. 6d.

Gulliver's Travels. With 88 Engravings by MORTEN. *Cheap Edition.* Cloth, 3s. 6d. ; cloth gilt, 5s.

Gum Boughs and Wattle Bloom, Gathered on Australian Hills and Plains. By DONALD MACDONALD. 5s.

Gun and its Development, The. By W. W. GREENER. With 500 Illustrations. 10s. 6d.

Guns, Modern Shot. By W. W. GREENER. Illustrated. 5s.

Health at School. By CLEMENT DUKES, M.D., B.S. 7s. 6d.

Health, The Book of. By Eminent Physicians and Surgeons. Cloth, 21s. ; Roxburgh, 25s.

Health, The Influence of Clothing on. By F. TREVES, F.R.G.S. 2s.

Heavens, The Story of the. By Sir ROBERT STAWELL BALL, LL.D., F.R.S., F.R.A.S. With Coloured Plates and Wood Engravings. 31s. 6d.

Heroes of Britain in Peace and War. In Two Vols., with 300 Original Illustrations. 5s. each ; or One Vol., library binding, 10s. 6d.

Holiday Studies of Wordsworth : by Rivers, Woods, and Alps, The Wharfe, The Duddon, and the Stelvio Pass. By the Rev. F. A. MALLESON, M.A. 5s.

Homes, Our, and How to Make them Healthy. By Eminent Authorities. Illustrated. 15s.

Horse, The Book of the. By SAMUEL SIDNEY. With 28 Fac-simile Coloured Plates. *Enlarged Edition.* Demy 4to, 35s.; half-morocco, 45s.

Household, Cassell's Book of the. Vols. I. and II., 5s. each.

Household Guide, Cassell's. Illustrated. Four Vols., 20s.

How Women may Earn a Living. By MERCY GROGAN. 6d.

India, Cassell's History of. By JAMES GRANT. With about 400 Illustrations. Library binding. One Vol. 15s.

Irish Union, The ; Before and After. By A. K. CONNELL, M.A. 2s. 6d.

John Orlebar, Clk. By the Author of " Culmshire Folk." 2s.

John Parmelee's Curse. By JULIAN HAWTHORNE. 2s. 6d.

Karmel the Scout. A Novel. By SYLVANUS COBB, Junr. Cloth, 3s. 6d.

Kennel Guide, The Practical. By Dr. GORDON STABLES. 1s.

Khiva, A Ride to. By Col. FRED. BURNABY. 1s. 6d.

Kidnapped. By R. L. STEVENSON. *Illustrated Edition.* 5s.

King Solomon's Mines. By H. RIDER HAGGARD. *Illustrated Edition.* 5s.

Ladies' Physician, The. A Guide for Women in the Treatment of their Ailments. By a Physician. 6s.

Lady Biddy Fane, The Admirable. By FRANK BARRETT. 5s.

Landscape Painting in Oils, A Course of Lessons in. By A. F. GRACE. With Nine Reproductions in Colour. *Cheap Edition,* 25s.

Law, How to Avoid. By A. J. WILLIAMS, M.P. 1s. *Cheap Edition.*

Legends for Lionel. By WALTER CRANE. Coloured Illustrations. 5s.

Letts's Diaries and other Time-saving Publications are now published exclusively by CASSELL & COMPANY. (*A list free on application.*)

Life Assurance, Medical Handbook of. By JAMES EDWARD POLLOCK, M.D., and JAMES CHISHOLM. 7s. 6d.

Local Government in England and Germany. By the Right Hon. Sir ROBERT MORIER, G.C.B., &c. 1s.

London (Ancient and Modern). From the Sanitary and Medical Point of View. By G. V. POORE, M.D., F.R.C.P. Illustrated. 5s.

London, Greater. By EDWARD WALFORD. Two Vols. With about 400 Illustrations. 9s. each.

London, Old and New. Six Vols., each containing about 200 Illustrations and Maps. Cloth, 9s. each.

Longfellow's Poetical Works. Illustrated, £3 3s.; *Popular Edition,* 16s.

Master of Ballantrae, The. By ROBERT LOUIS STEVENSON. 5s.

Mechanics, The Practical Dictionary of. Containing 15,000 Drawings. Four Vols. 21s. each.

Medicine, Manuals for Students of. (*A List forwarded post free.*)

Metropolitan Year-Book, The. Paper, 5s.; cloth, 5s. 6d.

Metzerott, Shoemaker. Cr. 8vo, 5s.

Milton's L'Allegro and Il Penseroso. Fully Illustrated. Cloth, 2s. 6d.

Modern Europe, A History of. By C. A. FYFFE, M.A. Complete in Three Vols. 12s. each.

Music, Illustrated History of. By EMIL NAUMANN. Edited by the Rev. Sir F. A. GORE OUSELEY, Bart. Illustrated. Two Vols. 31s. 6d.

National Library, Cassell's. In Volumes, each containing about 192 pages. Paper covers, 3d.; cloth, 6d. (*A Complete List of the Volumes will be sent post free on application.*)

Natural History, Cassell's Concise. By F. PERCEVAL WRIGHT, M.A., M.D., F.L.S. With several Hundred Illustrations. 7s. 6d.

Natural History, Cassell's New. Edited by Prof. P. MARTIN DUNCAN, M.B., F.R.S., F.G.S. Complete in Six Vols. With about 2,000 Illustrations. Cloth, 9s. each.

Nursing for the Home and for the Hospital, A Handbook of. By CATHERINE J. WOOD. *Cheap Edition.* 1s. 6d.; cloth, 2s.

Nursing of Sick Children, A Handbook for the. By CATHERINE J. WOOD. 2s. 6d.

Oil Painting, A Manual of. By the Hon. JOHN COLLIER. 2s. 6d.

Our Own Country. Six Vols. With 1,200 Illustrations. 7s. 6d. each.

Painting, Practical Guides to. With Coloured Plates and full instructions :—

MARINE PAINTING. 5s.	TREE PAINTING. 5s.
ANIMAL PAINTING. 5s.	WATER-COLOUR PAINTING. 5s.
CHINA PAINTING. 5s.	NEUTRAL TINT. 5s.
FIGURE PAINTING. 7s. 6d.	SEPIA, in Two Vols., 3s. each; or
ELEMENTARY FLOWER PAINTING. 3s.	in One Vol., 5s.
FLOWER PAINTING, Two Books, 5s. each.	FLOWERS, AND HOW TO PAINT THEM. 5s.

Paxton's Flower Garden. By Sir JOSEPH PAXTON and Prof. LINDLEY. Three Vols. With 100 Coloured Plates. £1 1s. each.

People I've Smiled with. By MARSHALL P. WILDER. 2s.; cloth, 2s. 6d.

Peoples of the World, The. In Six Vols. By Dr. ROBERT BROWN. Illustrated. 7s. 6d. each.

Phantom City, The. By W. WESTALL. 5s.

Photography for Amateurs. By T. C. HEPWORTH. Illustrated. 1s.; or cloth, 1s. 6d.

Phrase and Fable, Dictionary of. By the Rev. Dr. BREWER. *Cheap Edition, Enlarged,* cloth, 3s. 6d.; or with leather back, 4s. 6d.

Picturesque America. Complete in Four Vols., with 48 Exquisite Steel Plates and about 800 Original Wood Engravings. £2 2s. each.

Picturesque Australasia, Cassell's. With upwards of 250 Illustrations. Vol. I., 7s. 6d.

Picturesque Canada. With 600 Original Illustrations. 2 Vols. £3 3s. each.

Picturesque Europe. Complete in Five Vols. Each containing 13 Exquisite Steel Plates, from Original Drawings, and nearly 200 Original Illustrations. ORIGINAL EDITION. Cloth, £21; half morocco, £31 10s.; morocco gilt, £52 10s. The POPULAR EDITION is published in Five Vols., 18s. each.

Pigeon Keeper, The Practical. By LEWIS WRIGHT. Illustrated. 3s. 6d.

Pigeons, The Book of. By ROBERT FULTON. Edited and Arranged by L. WRIGHT. With 50 Coloured Plates, 31s. 6d.; half-morocco, £2 2s.

Poets, Cassell's Miniature Library of the :—

BURNS. Two Vols. 2s. 6d.	MILTON. Two Vols. 2s. 6d.
BYRON. Two Vols. 2s. 6d.	SCOTT. Two Vols. 2s. 6d. [2s. 6d.
HOOD. Two Vols. 2s. 6d.	SHERIDAN and GOLDSMITH. 2 Vols.
LONGFELLOW. Two Vols. 2s. 6d.	WORDSWORTH. Two Vols. 2s. 6d.

SHAKESPEARE. Illustrated. In 12 Vols., in Case, 12s.

Police Code, and Manual of the Criminal Law. By C. E. HOWARD VINCENT, M.P. 2s.

Polytechnic Series, The.
> Forty Lessons in Carpentry Workshop Practice. Cloth gilt, 1s.
> Practical Plane and Solid Geometry, including Graphic Arithmetic. Vol. I., Elementary Stage. Cloth gilt, 3s.
> Forty Lessons in Engineering Workshop Practice. 1s. 6d.
> Technical Scales. Set of Ten in cloth case, 1s.
> Elementary Chemistry for Science Schools and Classes. Crown 8vo, 1s. 6d.

Pope and the New Era, The. Being Letters from the Vatican in 1889. By WILLIAM T. STEAD, Author of "Truth about Russia." 6s.

Popular Library, Cassell's. Cloth, 1s. each.

The Russian Empire.	The Story of the English Jacobins.
The Religious Revolution in the 16th Century.	Domestic Folk Lore.
	The Rev. Rowland Hill: Preacher and Wit.
English Journalism.	Boswell and Johnson: their Companions and Contemporaries.
Our Colonial Empire.	
The Young Man in the Battle of Life.	History of the Free-Trade Movement in England.

Poultry Keeper, The Practical. By LEWIS WRIGHT. With Coloured Plates and Illustrations. 3s. 6d.

Poultry, The Book of. By LEWIS WRIGHT. *Popular Edition.* 10s. 6d.

Poultry, The Illustrated Book of. By LEWIS WRIGHT. With Fifty Coloured Plates. Cloth, 31s. 6d. ; half-morocco, £2 2s.

Pre-Raphaelites, The Italian, in the National Gallery. By COSMO MONKHOUSE. Illustrated. 1s.

Queen Victoria, The Life and Times of. By ROBERT WILSON. Complete in Two Vols. With numerous Illustrations. 9s. each.

Quiver, The. Yearly Volume. Illustrated. 7s. 6d.

Rabbit-Keeper, The Practical. By CUNICULUS. Illustrated. 3s. 6d.

Railway Guides, Official Illustrated. With Illustrations, Maps, &c. Price 1s. each ; or in cloth, 2s. each.
> GREAT NORTHERN RAILWAY.
> GREAT WESTERN RAILWAY. *Revised and Enlarged.*
> LONDON, BRIGHTON AND SOUTH COAST RAILWAY.
> LONDON AND NORTH-WESTERN RAILWAY. *Revised and Enlarged.*
> LONDON AND SOUTH-WESTERN RAILWAY.
> MIDLAND RAILWAY.
> SOUTH-EASTERN RAILWAY.

Railway Library, Cassell's. Crown 8vo, boards, 2s. each.

UNDER A STRANGE MASK. By FRANK BARRETT.	THE YOKE OF THE THORAM. By SIDNEY LUSKA.
THE COOMBSBERROW MYSTERY. By JAMES COLWALL.	WHO IS JOHN NOMAN? By CHARLES HENRY BECKETT.
DEAD MAN'S ROCK. By Q.	
A QUEER RACE. By W. WESTALL.	THE TRAGEDY OF BRINKWATER. By MARTHA L. MOODEY.
CAPTAIN TRAFALGAR. By WESTALL and LAURIE.	
THE PHANTOM CITY. By W. WESTALL.	AN AMERICAN PENMAN. By JULIAN HAWTHORNE.
** The above can also be obtained in cloth, 2s. 6d. each.	SECTION 558; or, THE FATAL LETTER. By JULIAN HAWTHORNE.
JACK GORDON, KNIGHT ERRANT, GOTHAM, 1883. By BARCLAY NORTH.	THE BROWN STONE BOY. By W. H. BISHOP.
THE DIAMOND BUTTON. By BARCLAY NORTH.	A TRAGIC MYSTERY. By JULIAN HAWTHORNE.
ANOTHER'S CRIME. By JULIAN HAWTHORNE.	THE GREAT BANK ROBBERY. By JULIAN HAWTHORNE.

Richard, Henry, M.P. A Biography. By CHARLES S. MIALL. 7s. 6d.

Rivers of Great Britain, The : Descriptive, Historical, Pictorial. RIVERS OF THE EAST COAST. 42s.

Rossetti, Dante Gabriel, as Designer and Writer. Notes by WILLIAM MICHAEL ROSSETTI. 7s. 6d.

Royal River, The: The Thames, from Source to Sea. With Descriptive Text and a Series of beautiful Engravings. £2 2s.

Russia. By Sir DONALD MACKENZIE WALLACE, M.A. 5s.

Russia, Truth About. By W. T. STEAD. 8vo, cloth, 10s. 6d.

Russo-Turkish War, Cassell's History of. With about 500 Illustrations. Two Vols., 9s. each.

Red Library, Cassell's. Stiff covers, 1s. each; cloth, 2s. each.

Jane Eyre.	Ivanhoe.	Poe's Works.
Wuthering Heights.	Oliver Twist.	Old Mortality.
Dombey and Son	Selections from Hood's	The Hour and the Man.
(Two Vols.).	Works.	Handy Andy.
The Prairie.	Longfellow's Prose	Scarlet Letter.
Night and Morning.	Works.	Pickwick (Two Vols.).
Kenilworth.	Sense and Sensibility.	Last of the Mohicans.
The Ingoldsby Legends.	Lytton's Plays.	Pride and Prejudice.
	Tales, Poems, and	Yellowplush Papers.
The Tower of London.	Sketches. Bret Harte	Tales of the Borders.
	Martin Chuzzlewit	Last Days of Palmyra.
The Pioneers.	(Two Vols.).	Washington Irving's
Charles O'Malley.	The Prince of the	Sketch-Book.
Barnaby Rudge.	House of David.	The Talisman.
Cakes and Ale.	Sheridan's Plays.	Rienzi.
The King's Own.	Uncle Tom's Cabin.	Old Curiosity Shop.
People I have Met.	Deerslayer.	Heart of Midlothian.
The Pathfinder.	Eugene Aram.	Last Days of Pompeii.
Evelina.	Jack Hinton.	American Humour.
Scott's Poems.	Rome and the Early	Sketches by Boz.
Last of the Barons.	Christians.	Macaulay's Lays and
Adventures of Mr.	The Trials of Margaret Lyndsay.	Essays.
Ledbury.		Harry Lorrequer.

St. Cuthbert's Tower. By FLORENCE WARDEN. *Cheap Edition.* 5s.

Salads: the best Salad Plants, and the best ways of Mixing a Salad. By HENRY F. MOORE and M. VILMORIN. Cr. 8vo, 1s. 6d.

Saturday Journal, Cassell's. Yearly Volume, cloth, 7s. 6d.

Science for All. Edited by Dr. ROBERT BROWN. *Revised Edition.* Illustrated. Five Vols. 9s. each.

Scouting for Stanley in East Africa: a Record of the Adventures of Thomas Stevens in Search of H. M. Stanley. With 14 Illustrations. Cloth, 7s. 6d.

Sculpture, A Primer of. By E. ROSCOE MULLINS. With Illustrations. 2s. 6d.

Sea, The: Its Stirring Story of Adventure, Peril, and Heroism. By F. WHYMPER. With 400 Illustrations. Four Vols., 7s. 6d. each.

Secret of the Lamas, The. A Tale of Thibet. Crown 8vo, 5s.

Shaftesbury, The Seventh Earl of, K.G., The Life and Work of. By EDWIN HODDER. Three Vols., 36s. *Popular Edition.* One Vol., 7s. 6d.

Shakespeare, The Plays of. Edited by Professor HENRY MORLEY. Complete in 13 Vols., cloth, 21s.

Shakespeare, Cassell's Quarto Edition. Containing about 600 Illustrations by H. C. SELOUS. Complete in Three Vols., cloth gilt, £3 3s.

Shakespeare, Miniature. Illustrated. In Twelve Vols., in box, 12s.; or in Red Paste Grain (box to match), with spring catch, 21s.

Shakespeare, The England of. By E. GOADBY. Illustrated. 2s. 6d.

Shakspere, The International. *Edition de Luxe.*

"KING HENRY IV." Illustrated by EDUARD GRÜTZNER, £3 10s.
"AS YOU LIKE IT." Illustrated by ÉMILE BAYARD, £3 10s.
"ROMEO AND JULIET." Illustrated by F. DICKSEE, A.R.A., £3 5s.

Shakspere, The Leopold. With 400 Illustrations. *Cheap Edition.* 3s. 6d. Cloth gilt, 6s.; Roxburgh, 7s. 6d.

Shakspere, The Royal. With Steel Plates and Wood Engravings. Three Vols. 15s. each.

Sketching from Nature in Water Colours. By AARON PENLEY. With Illustrations in Chromo-Lithography. 15s.

Social Welfare, Subjects of. By the Rt. Hon. Sir LYON PLAYFAIR, K.C.B. 7s. 6d.

Splendid Spur, The. Edited by Q. 5s.

Sports and Pastimes, Cassell's Complete Book of. *Cheap Edition.* With more than 900 Illustrations. Medium 8vo, 992 pages, cloth, 3s. 6d.

Star-Land. By Sir ROBERT STAWELL BALL, LL.D., F.R.S., F.R A.S. Illustrated. Crown 8vo, 6s.

Steam Engine, The. By W. H. NORTHCOTT, C.E. 3s. 6d.

Strange Doings in Strange Places. Complete Sensational Stories by FRANK BARRETT, "Q," G. MANVILLE FENN, &c. &c. Cr. 8vo, 5s.

Technical Education. By F. C. MONTAGUE. 6d.

Thackeray, Character Sketches from. Six New and Original Drawings by FREDERICK BARNARD, reproduced in Photogravure. 21s.

Treasure Island. By R. L. STEVENSON. Illustrated. 5s.

Trees, Familiar. By G. S. BOULGER, F.L.S. Two Series. With 40 full-page Coloured Plates by W. H. J. BOOT. 12s. 6d. each.

Troy Town, The Astonishing History of. By Q. 5s.

Two Women or One? From the Manuscripts of Doctor LEONARD BENARY. By HENRY HARLAND. 1s.

"Unicode": the Universal Telegraphic Phrase Book. *Desk or Pocket Edition.* 2s. 6d.

United States, Cassell's History of the. By the late EDMUND OLLIER. With 600 Illustrations. Three Vols. 9s. each.

United States, Youth's History of the. Illustrated. 4 Volumes. 36s.

Universal History, Cassell's Illustrated. Four Vols. 9s. each.

Verdict, The. A Tract on the Political Significance of the Report of the Parnell Commission. By Prof. A. V. DICEY, Q.C. 2s. 6d.

Vicar of Wakefield and other Works by OLIVER GOLDSMITH. Illustrated. 3s. 6d.; cloth, gilt edges, 5s.

What Girls Can Do. By PHYLLIS BROWNE. 2s. 6d.

Wild Birds, Familiar. By W. SWAYSLAND. Four Series. With 40 Coloured Plates in each. 12s. 6d. each.

Wild Flowers, Familiar. By F. E. HULME, F.L.S., F.S.A. Five Series. With 40 Coloured Plates in each. 12s. 6d. each.

Woman's World, The. Yearly Volume. 18s.

Wood, Rev. J. G., Life of the. By the Rev. THEODORE WOOD. Demy 8vo, cloth, price 10s. 6d.

Work. An Illustrated Magazine of Practice and Theory for all Workmen, Professional and Amateur. Yearly Vol., 7s. 6d.

World of Wit and Humour, The. With 400 Illustrations. Cloth, 7s. 6d.; cloth gilt, gilt edges, 10s. 6d.

World of Wonders. Two Vols. With 400 Illustrations. 7s. 6d. each.

Yule Tide. Cassell's Christmas Annual, 1s.

ILLUSTRATED MAGAZINES.

The Quiver. ENLARGED SERIES. Monthly, 6d.
Cassell's Family Magazine. Monthly, 7d.
"Little Folks" Magazine. Monthly, 6d.
The Magazine of Art. Monthly, 1s.
The Woman's World. Monthly, 1s.
Cassell's Saturday Journal. Weekly, 1d.; Monthly, 6d.
Work. Weekly, 1d.; Monthly, 6d.

Bibles and Religious Works.

Bible, Cassell's Illustrated Family. With 900 Illustrations. Leather, gilt edges, £2 10s.

Bible Dictionary, Cassell's. With nearly 600 Illustrations. 7s. 6d.

Bible Educator, The. Edited by the Very Rev. Dean PLUMPTRE, D.D., Wells. With Illustrations, Maps, &c. Four Vols., cloth, 6s. each.

Bible Student in the British Museum, The. By the Rev. J. G. KITCHIN, M.A. 1s.

Biblewomen and Nurses. Yearly Volume. Illustrated. 3s.

Bunyan's Pilgrim's Progress (Cassell's Illustrated). 4to. 7s. 6d.

Bunyan's Pilgrim's Progress. With Illustrations. Cloth, 3s. 6d.

Child's Bible, The. With 200 Illustrations. 150th Thousand. 7s. 6d.

Child's Life of Christ, The. With 200 Illustrations. 7s. 6d.

"Come, ye Children." Illustrated. By Rev. BENJAMIN WAUGH. 5s.

Doré Bible. With 238 Illustrations by GUSTAVE DORÉ. Small folio, cloth, £8; best morocco, gilt edges, £15.

Early Days of Christianity, The. By the Ven. Archdeacon FARRAR, D.D., F.R.S.
LIBRARY EDITION. Two Vols., 24s.; morocco, £2 2s.
POPULAR EDITION. Complete in One Volume, cloth, 6s.; cloth, gilt edges, 7s. 6d.; Persian morocco, 10s. 6d.; tree-calf, 15s.

Family Prayer-Book, The. Edited by Rev. Canon GARBETT, M.A., and Rev. S. MARTIN. Extra crown 4to, cloth, 5s.; morocco, 18s.

Glories of the Man of Sorrows, The. Sermons preached at St. James's, Piccadilly. By Rev. H. G. BONAVIA HUNT, Mus.D., F.R.S., Ed. 2s. 6d.

"Heart Chords." A Series of Works by Eminent Divines. Bound in cloth, red edges, One Shilling each.

MY BIBLE. By the Right Rev. W. BOYD CARPENTER, Bishop of Ripon.
MY FATHER. By the Right Rev. ASHTON OXENDEN, late Bishop of Montreal.
MY WORK FOR GOD. By the Right Rev. Bishop COTTERILL.
MY OBJECT IN LIFE. By the Ven. Archdeacon FARRAR, D.D.
MY ASPIRATIONS. By the Rev. G. MATHESON, D.D.
MY EMOTIONAL LIFE. By the Rev. Preb. CHADWICK, D.D.
MY BODY. By the Rev. Prof. W. G. BLAIKIE, D.D.

MY GROWTH IN DIVINE LIFE. By the Rev. Preb. REYNOLDS, M.A.
MY SOUL. By the Rev. P. B. POWER, M.A.
MY HEREAFTER. By the Very Rev. Dean BICKERSTETH.
MY WALK WITH GOD. By the Very Rev. Dean MONTGOMERY.
MY AIDS TO THE DIVINE LIFE. By the Very Rev Dean BOYLE.
MY SOURCES OF STRENGTH. By the Rev. E. E. JENKINS, M.A., Secretary of Wesleyan Missionary Society.

Helps to Belief. A Series of Helpful Manuals on the Religious Difficulties of the Day. Edited by the Rev. TEIGNMOUTH SHORE, M.A., Chaplain-in-Ordinary to the Queen. Cloth, 1s. each.

CREATION. By the Lord Bishop of Carlisle.
THE DIVINITY OF OUR LORD. By the Lord Bishop of Derry.
THE MORALITY OF THE OLD TESTAMENT. By the Rev. Newman Smyth, D.D.

MIRACLES. By the Rev. Brownlow Maitland, M.A.
PRAYER. By the Rev. T. Teignmouth Shore. M.A.
THE ATONEMENT. By the Lord Bishop of Peterborough.

Holy Land and the Bible, The. By the Rev. CUNNINGHAM GEIKIE, D.D. Two Vols., with Map, 24s.

"I Must." Short Missionary Bible Readings. By SOPHIA M. NUGENT. Enamelled covers, 6d.; cloth, gilt edges, 1s.

Life of Christ, The. By the Ven. Archdeacon FARRAR, D.D., F.R.S.
ILLUSTRATED EDITION, with about 300 Original Illustrations.
Extra crown 4to, cloth, gilt edges, 21s. ; morocco antique, 42s.
LIBRARY EDITION. Two Vols. Cloth, 24s. ; morocco, 42s.
POPULAR EDITION, in One Vol. 8vo, cloth, 6s. ; cloth, gilt edges,
7s. 6d. ; Persian morocco, gilt edges, 10s. 6d. ; tree-calf, 15s.

Marriage Ring, The. By WILLIAM LANDELS, D.D. *New and
Cheaper Edition.* 3s. 6d.

Moses and Geology ; or, The Harmony of the Bible with Science.
By the Rev. SAMUEL KINNS, Ph.D., F.R.A.S. Illustrated. *Cheap
Edition,* 6s.

New Testament Commentary for English Readers, The. Edited
by the Rt. Rev. C. J. ELLICOTT, D.D., Lord Bishop of Gloucester
and Bristol. In Three Volumes, 21s. each.
Vol. I.—The Four Gospels.
Vol. II.—The Acts, Romans, Corinthians, Galatians.
Vol. III.—The remaining Books of the New Testament.

New Testament Commentary. Edited by Bishop ELLICOTT. Handy
Volume Edition. St. Matthew, 3s. 6d. St. Mark, 3s. St. Luke,
3s. 6d. St. John, 3s. 6d. The Acts of the Apostles, 3s. 6d. Romans,
2s. 6d. Corinthians I. and II., 3s. Galatians, Ephesians, and Philip-
pians, 3s. Colossians, Thessalonians, and Timothy, 3s. Titus,
Philemon, Hebrews, and James, 3s. Peter, Jude, and John, 3s.
The Revelation, 3s. An Introduction to the New Testament, 3s. 6d.

Old Testament Commentary for English Readers, The. Edited
by the Right Rev. C. J. ELLICOTT, D.D., Lord Bishop of Gloucester
and Bristol. Complete in 5 Vols., 21s. each.
Vol. I.—Genesis to Numbers. | Vol. III.—Kings I. to Esther.
Vol. II.—Deuteronomy to | Vol. IV.—Job to Isaiah.
Samuel II. | Vol. V.—Jeremiah to Malachi.

Old Testament Commentary. Edited by Bishop ELLICOTT. Handy
Volume Edition. Genesis, 3s. 6d. Exodus, 3s. Leviticus, 3s.
Numbers, 2s. 6d. Deuteronomy, 2s. 6d.

Protestantism, The History of. By the Rev. J. A. WYLIE, LL.D.
Containing upwards of 600 Original Illustrations. Three Vols., 9s. each.

Quiver Yearly Volume, The. 250 high-class Illustrations. 7s. 6d.

Religion, The Dictionary of. By the Rev. W. BENHAM, B.D. 21s. ;
Roxburgh, 25s.

St. George for England ; and other Sermons preached to Children. By
the Rev. T. TEIGNMOUTH SHORE, M.A. 5s.

St. Paul, The Life and Work of. By the Ven. Archdeacon FARRAR,
D.D., F.R.S., Chaplain-in-Ordinary to the Queen.
LIBRARY EDITION. Two Vols., cloth, 24s. ; calf, 42s.
ILLUSTRATED EDITION, complete in One Volume, with about 300
Illustrations, £1 1s. ; morocco, £2 2s.
POPULAR EDITION. One Volume, 8vo, cloth, 6s. ; cloth, gilt edges,
7s. 6d. ; Persian morocco, 10s. 6d. ; tree-calf, 15s.

Secular Life, The Gospel of the. Sermons preached at Oxford. By
the Hon. Canon FREMANTLE. *Cheaper Edition.* 2s. 6d.

Shall We Know One Another ? By the Rt. Rev. J. C. RYLE, D.D.,
Bishop of Liverpool. *New and Enlarged Edition.* Cloth limp, 1s.

Stromata. By the Ven. Archdeacon SHERRINGHAM, M.A. 2s. 6d.

"Sunday," Its Origin, History, and Present Obligation. By the
Ven. Archdeacon HESSEY, D.C.L. *Fifth Edition.* 7s. 6d.

Twilight of Life, The. Words of Counsel and Comfort for the
Aged. By the Rev. JOHN ELLERTON, M.A. 1s. 6d.

Voice of Time, The. By JOHN STROUD. Cloth gilt, 1s.

Educational Works and Students' Manuals.

Alphabet, Cassell's Pictorial. 3s. 6d.

Arithmetics, The Modern School. By GEORGE RICKS, B.Sc. Lond. With Test Cards. (*List on application.*)

Book-Keeping. By THEODORE JONES. For Schools, 2s. ; cloth, 3s. For the Million, 2s. ; cloth, 3s. Books for Jones's System. 2s.

Chemistry, The Public School. By J. H. ANDERSON, M.A. 2s. 6d.

Copy-Books, Cassell's Graduated. *Eighteen Books.* 2d. each.

Copy-Books, The Modern School. *Twelve Books.* 2d. each.

Drawing Copies, Cassell's Modern School Freehand. First Grade, 1s. ; Second Grade, 2s.

Drawing Copies, Cassell's "New Standard." *Fourteen Books.* Books A to F for Standards I. to IV., 2d. each. Books G, H, K, L, M, O, for Standards V. to VII., 3d. each. Books N and P, 4d. each.

Electricity, Practical. By Prof. W. E. AYRTON. 7s. 6d.

Energy and Motion. By WILLIAM PAICE, M.A. Illustrated. 1s. 6d.

English Literature, First Sketch of. *New and Enlarged Edition.* By Prof. MORLEY. 7s. 6d.

English Literature, The Story of. By ANNA BUCKLAND. 3s. 6d.

Euclid, Cassell's. Edited by Prof. WALLACE, M.A. 1s.

Euclid, The First Four Books of. In paper, 6d. ; cloth, 9d.

Experimental Geometry. By PAUL BERT. Illustrated. 1s. 6d.

French, Cassell's Lessons in. *New and Revised Edition.* Parts I. and II., each 2s. 6d. ; complete, 4s. 6d. Key, 1s. 6d.

French-English and English-French Dictionary. *Entirely New and Enlarged Edition.* 1,150 pages, 8vo, cloth, 3s. 6d.

French Reader, Cassell's Public School. By G. S. CONRAD. 2s. 6d.

Galbraith and Haughton's Scientific Manuals. By the Rev. Prof. GALBRAITH, M.A., and the Rev. Prof. HAUGHTON, M.D., D.C.I. Plane Trigonometry, 2s. 6d.—Euclid, Books I., II., III., 2s. 6d.—Books IV., V., VI., 2s. 6d.—Mathematical Tables, 3s. 6d.—Mechanics, 3s. 6d. —Natural Philosophy, 3s. 6d.—Optics, 2s. 6d.—Hydrostatics, 3s. 6d.— Astronomy, 5s.—Steam Engine, 3s. 6d.—Algebra. Part I., cloth, 2s. 6d.; Complete, 7s. 6d.—Tides and Tidal Currents, with Tidal Cards, 3s.

German Dictionary, Cassell's New. German-English, English-German. Cloth, 7s. 6d. ; half-morocco, 9s.

German of To-Day. By Dr. HEINEMANN. 1s. 6d.

German Reading, First Lessons in. By A. JAGST. Illustrated. 1s.

Hand-and-Eye Training. By G. RICKS, B.Sc. Two Vols., with 16 Coloured Plates in each Vol. Crown 4to, 6s. each.

Handbook of New Code of Regulations. *New and Revised Edition.* By JOHN F. MOSS. 1s. ; cloth, 2s.

Historical Cartoons, Cassell's Coloured. Size 45 in. × 35 in., 2s. each. Mounted on canvas and varnished, with rollers, 5s. each.

Historical Course for Schools, Cassell's. Illustrated throughout. I.—Stories from English History, 1s. II.—The Simple Outline of English History, 1s. 3d. III.—The Class History of England, 2s. 6d.

Horati Opera. With Preface, Conspectus Metrorum, Index Nominum et Rerum Memorabilium, and Critical Notes. 3s.

Homer, The Iliad of. Complete Text. With a Preface and Summary. Two Vols. Vol. I., 3s. ; Vol. II., 3s. 6d.

Latin-English and English-Latin Dictionary. By J. R. BEARD, D.D., and C. BEARD, B.A. Crown 8vo, 914 pp., 3s. 6d.

Latin-English Dictionary, Cassell's. By J. R. V. MARCHANT, 3s. 6d.

Latin Primer, The First. By Prof. POSTGATE. 1s.

Latin Primer, The New. By Prof. J. P. POSTGATE. Crown 8vo, 2s. 6d.

Latin Prose for Lower Forms. By M. A. BAYFIELD, M.A. 2s. 6d.

Laws of Every-Day Life. By H. O. ARNOLD-FORSTER. 1s. 6d.

Little Folks' History of England. Illustrated. 1s. 6d.

Making of the Home, The: A Book of Domestic Economy for School and Home Use. By Mrs. SAMUEL A. BARNETT. 1s. 6d.

Marlborough Books:—Arithmetic Examples, 3s. Arithmetic Rules, 1s. 6d. French Exercises, 3s. 6d. French Grammar, 2s. 6d. German do., 3s. 6d.

Mechanics and Machine Design, Numerical Examples in Practical. By R. G. BLAINE, M.E. With Diagrams. Cloth, 2s. 6d.

"Model Joint" Wall Sheets, for Instruction in Manual Training. By S. BARTER. Eight Sheets, 2s. 6d. each.

Music, An Elementary Manual of. By HENRY LESLIE. 1s.

Object Lessons from Nature. By Prof. L. C. MIALL, F.L.S. 2s. 6d.

Popular Educator, Cassell's NEW. With Revised Text, New Maps, New Coloured Plates, New Type, &c. To be completed in 8 Vols. 5s. each.

Popular Educator, Cassell's. Complete in Six Vols., 5s. each.

Readers, Cassell's "Higher Class." (*List on application.*)

Readers, Cassell's Historical. Illustrated throughout, printed on superior paper, and strongly bound in cloth. (*List on application.*)

Readers, Cassell's Readable. Carefully graduated, extremely interesting, and illustrated throughout. (*List on application.*)

Readers for Infant Schools, Coloured. Three Books. 4d. each.

Reader, The Citizen. By H. O. ARNOLD-FORSTER. Illustrated. 1s. 6d.

Reader, The Temperance. By Rev. J. DENNIS HIRD. Cr. 8vo, 1s. 6d.

Readers, The "Modern School" Geographical. (*List on application.*)

Readers, The "Modern School." Illustrated. (*List on application.*)

Reckoning, Howard's Anglo-American Art of. By C. FRUSHER HOWARD. Paper covers, 1s.; cloth, 2s.

Science Applied to Work. By J. A. BOWER. 1s.

Science of Everyday Life. By JOHN A. BOWER. Illustrated. 1s.

Shakspere's Plays for School Use. 5 Books. Illustrated, 6d. each.

Shakspere Reading Book, The. Illustrated. 3s. 6d.

Spelling, A Complete Manual of. By J. D. MORELL, LL.D. 1s.

Technical Manuals, Cassell's. Illustrated throughout:—
Handrailing and Staircasing, 3s. 6d.—Bricklayers, Drawing for, 3s.—Building Construction, 2s.- Cabinet-Makers, Drawing for, 3s.—Carpenters and Joiners, Drawing for, 3s. 6d.—Gothic Stonework, 3s.—Linear Drawing and Practical Geometry, 2s.—Linear Drawing and Projection, The Two Vols. in One, 3s. 6d.—Machinists and Engineers, Drawing for, 4s. 6d.—Metal-Plate Workers, Drawing for, 3s.—Model Drawing, 3s.—Orthographical and Isometrical Projection, 2s.—Practical Perspective, 3s.- Stonemasons, Drawing for, 3s.—Applied Mechanics, by Sir R. S. Ball, LL.D., 2s.—Systematic Drawing and Shading, 2s.

Technical Educator, Cassell's. *Revised Edition.* Four Vols., 5s. each.

Technology, Manuals of. Edited by Prof. AYRTON, F.R.S., and RICHARD WORMELL, D.Sc., M.A. Illustrated throughout:—
The Dyeing of Textile Fabrics, by Prof. Hummel, 5s.—Watch and Clock Making, by D. Glasgow, 4s. 6d.—Steel and Iron, by Prof. W. H. Greenwood, F.C.S., M.I.C.E., &c., 5s.—Spinning Woollen and Worsted, by W. S. B. McLaren, M.P., 4s. 6d.—Design in Textile Fabrics, by T. R. Ashenhurst, 4s. 6d.—Practical Mechanics, by Prof. Perry, M.E., 3s. 6d.—Cutting Tools Worked by Hand and Machine, by Prof. Smith, 3s. 6d. *A Prospectus on application.*

Test Cards, Cassell's Combination. In sets, 1s. each.

Test Cards, "Modern School," Cassell's. In Sets, 1s. each.

CASSELL & COMPANY, LIMITED, *Ludgate Hill, London.*

Books for Young People.

"**Little Folks**" Half-Yearly Volume. Containing 432 4to pages, with about 200 Illustrations, and Pictures in Colour. Boards, 3s. 6d.; cloth, 5s.

Bo-Peep. A Book for the Little Ones. With Original Stories and Verses. Illustrated throughout. Yearly Volume. Boards, 2s. 6d.; cloth, 3s. 6d.

Cassell's Pictorial Scrap Book, containing several thousand Pictures beautifully printed and handsomely bound in one large volume. Coloured boards, 15s.; cloth lettered, 21s. Also in Six Sectional Vols., 3s. 6d. each.

Flora's Feast. A Masque of Flowers. Penned and Pictured by WALTER CRANE. With 40 Pages in Colours. 5s.

Legends for Lionel. With 40 Illustrations in Colour, by WALTER CRANE. 5s.

Little Mother Bunch. By Mrs. MOLESWORTH. Illustrated. Cloth, 3s. 6d.

The New Children's Album. Fcap. 4to, 330 pages. Illustrated throughout. 3s. 6d.

The Tales of the Sixty Mandarins. By P. V. RAMASWAMI RAJU. With an Introduction by Prof. HENRY MORLEY. Illustrated. 5s.

Books for Young People. Illustrated. Cloth gilt, 5s. each.

The King's Command: A Story for Girls. by Maggie Symington.
Under Bayard's Banner. By Henry Frith.
The Romance of Invention. By James Burnley.

The Champion of Odin; or, Viking Life in the Days of Old. By J. Fred. Hodgetts.
Bound by a Spell; or, The Hunted Witch of the Forest. By the Hon. Mrs. Greene.

Books for Young People. Illustrated. Price 3s. 6d. each.

Polly: A New-Fashioned Girl. By L. T. Meade.
For Fortune and Glory: A Story of the Soudan War. By Lewis Hough.
"Follow My Leader." By Talbot Baines Reed. [Ptl.
The Cost of a Mistake. By Sarah Pitt.
A World of Girls: The Story of a School. By L. T. Meade.
Lost among White Africans. By David Ker.

The Palace Beautiful. By L. T. Meade.
Freedom's Sword: A Story of the Days of Wallace and Bruce. By Annie S. Swan.
On Board the "Esmeralda." By John C. Hutcheson.
In Quest of Gold. By A. St. Johnston.
For Queen and King. By Henry Frith.
Perils Afloat and Brigands Ashore. By Alfred Elwes.

Books for Young People. Price 2s. 6d. each.

Heroes of Every-day Life. By Laura Lane. Illustrated.
Decisive Events in History. By Thomas Archer. With Original Illustrations.
The True Robinson Crusoes.
Peeps Abroad for Folks at Home. Illustrated.

Early Explorers. By Thomas Frost.
Home Chat with our Young Folks. Illustrated throughout.
Jungle, Peak, and Plain. Illustrated throughout.
The World's Lumber-Room. By Selina Gaye.

The "Cross and Crown" Series. With Illustrations in each Book. 2s. 6d. each.

Strong to Suffer: A Story of the Jews. By E. Wynne.
Heroes of the Indian Empire; or, Stories of Valour and Victory. By Ernest Foster.
In Letters of Flame: A Story of the Waldenses. By C. L. Mateaux.
Through Trial to Triumph. By Madeline B. Hunt.

By Fire and Sword: A Story of the Huguenots. By Thomas Archer.
Adam Hepburn's Vow: A Tale of Kirk and Covenant. By Anne S. Swan.
No. XIII.; or, The Story of the Lost Vestal. A Tale of Early Christian Days. By Emma Marshall.

"Golden Mottoes" Series, The. Each Book containing 208 pages, with Four full-page Original Illustrations. Crown 8vo, cloth gilt, **2s.** each.

"Nil Desperandum." By the Rev. F. Langbridge, M.A.

"Bear and Forbear." By Sarah Pitt.

"Foremost if I Can." By Helen Atteridge.

"Honour is my Guide." By Jeanie Hering (Mrs. Adams-Acton).

"Aim at a Sure End." By Emily Searchfield.

"He Conquers who Endures." By the Author of "May Cunningham's Trial," &c.

Books for Children. In Illuminated boards, fully Illustrated.

Twilight Fancies. **2s. 6d.**
Cheerful Clatter. **3s. 6d.**

A Dozen and One. **5s.**
Bible Talks. **5s.**

Cassell's Picture Story Books. Each containing Sixty Pages of Pictures and Stories, &c. **6d.** each.

Little Talks.
Bright Stars.
Nursery Toys.
Pet's Posy.
Tiny Tales.

Daisy's Story Book.
Dot's Story Book.
A Nest of Stories.
Good-Night Stories.
Chats for Small Chatterers.

Auntie's Stories.
Birdie's Story Book.
Little Chimes.
A Sheaf of Tales.
Dewdrop Stories.

Cassell's Sixpenny Story Books. All Illustrated, and containing Interesting Stories by well-known writers.

The Smuggler's Cave.
Little Lizzie.
Little Bird, Life and Adventures of.
Luke Barnicott.

The Boat Club.
Little Pickles.
The Elchester College Boys.
My First Cruise.
The Little Peacemaker.

The Delft Jug.

Cassell's Shilling Story Books. All Illustrated, and containing Interesting Stories.

Bunty and the Boys.
The Heir of Elmdale.
The Mystery at Shoncliff School.
Claimed at Last, and Roy's Reward.
Thorns and Tangles.
The Cuckoo in the Robin's Nest.
John's Mistake.
The History of Five Little Pitchers.
Diamonds in the Sand.

Surly Bob.
The Giant's Cradle.
Shag and Doll.
Aunt Lucia's Locket.
The Magic Mirror.
The Cost of Revenge.
Clever Frank.
Among the Redskins.
The Ferryman of Brill.
Harry Maxwell.
A Banished Monarch.
Seventeen Cats.

Illustrated Books for the Little Ones. Containing interesting Stories. All Illustrated. **1s.** each ; cloth gilt, **1s. 6d.**

Scrambles and Scrapes.
Tittle Tattle Tales.
Up and Down the Garden.
All Sorts of Adventures.
Our Sunday Stories.
Our Holiday Hours.
Indoors and Out.
Some Farm Friends.

Wandering Ways.
Dumb Friends.
Those Golden Sands.
Little Mothers & their Children.
Our Pretty Pets.
Our Schoolday Hours.
Creatures Tame.
Creatures Wild.

Albums for Children. Price **3s. 6d.** each.

The New Children's Album. Illustrated throughout. Cloth.

The Album for Home, School, and Play. Containing Stories by Popular Authors. Set in bold type, and Illustrated throughout.

My Own Album of Animals. With Full-page Illustrations.

Picture Album of All Sorts. With Full-page Illustrations.

The Chit-Chat Album. Illustrated throughout.

www.ingramcontent.com/pod-product-compliance
Lightning Source LLC
Chambersburg PA
CBHW031156050726
47495CB00019B/2307